Blues in Small Doses

Short Stories

By: Gulfrey Clarke

Published by Cocoon Publishers

coCoOn
PUBLISHERS

Bern Switzerland

http://gulfreyc77.wix.com/gulfreyclarke

ISBN: 978-3-9524291-1-2

CONTENTS

from the unsightly, outrageous, chaos distributed across her bedroom's floor. "You stupid fucking dummies! Let's go! Out! You're leaving my goddamned house, now! Get up, now! I don't know where y'all get off at making yourselves so damn comfortable in my home." She savagely kicked Joe on one of his pain-ridden knees he was clutching. He jumped up with a start and promptly lost his footing once again and landed rather awkwardly.

Then she cruelly kicked and stomped Al in his head. With both of his eyes closed he begged, "No, no more, please! Just let me go this once, pleaseeee!" Turning slightly, she spotted Joe's expanding pee stain and froze horrified to a point where no sound came out save for the grinding of her teeth as her wildly flickering purple-green eyes grew big as a saucer.

"Oh my God, Missss...Thank you. Thanks for saving us, Ms. Jones. That bed-machine was trying to kill us. I swear to God!" yelled Joe.

"What the hell ya talking about? You nasty, funky, fuckers! Get-up-and-out, now! I shouldda killed both of you. Just look at what you filthy pigs have done to my carpet. You goddamn bastards!"

Though bloody and traumatized, but alive, they set off running hard and in earnest, bent on quickly reaching daylight. "Don't worry Madame, you'll find out real soon!" shouted Joe as they raced out the front iron gate slowly gaining on their truck now in motion; an effort which seemed to them like a unreachable task, as each of their pains continued to escalate.

Ms. Jones worked up a serious sweat over the course of the next ninety minutes meticulously removing the stains and repulsive scent of urine, blood and bone chips from her bronze color shag carpeted floor. Then still breathing hard from the release of years of pent-up sexual energy discharged while cleaning up the floors, she gave in to desire and sat first before

5

laying down across the new bed. Now, she knew what possessed her husband Ralph to making this purchase after laying on it just one time, yesterday. The feeling was intoxicating and seductively surreal. "A friendly hello, Ms. Jones, I'm Reggie. Welcome to the new arrangement, and I do hope you're enjoying laying on me, Sweetie. Ciao!"

"Oh, Yeeeeaaah! This is heavenly," she replied and then paused deep in thought, "Wait! Just-one-damned-minute! Who the hell was that that just spoke to me? Jenny, is that you? Did someone say something? Is someone here? Oh no. No, I knew it wasn't you Jenny. That wasn't your voice...I must be losing my mind." There was only absolute silence in its purest form, for the next three minutes. "Oh well," Ms. Jones continued, "probably it was just some built-in recording—a welcoming device. I can dig it, baby." Then like a joyful child, Ms. Jones chuckled loudly as she gave the controls a ferocious workout and climaxed under the force of the bed's tremendous vibrations shouting, "Thank you, Jesus!"

***

Swiftly, strong men gathered deep within the bowels of the Pentagon, in Arlington, Virginia. This marked the beginning of a top-secret conference to terminate with prejudice the Bed Patrol's Control Network. A top Army official quickly flipped through the information package he received and said, "So it was the genius of John Alan Hoover who gave beds power over us, was it not?"

"Well, let's not discount the fact that our peanut-farmer-president had a hand in it, sort of, too," replied Jim Pearson, Pentagon spokesman.

"Look! Let's get right down to the bottom of this. Spit it out!" said Jack Briscoe, a disgusted-looking four-star Navy General—

6

with that girdled six-month-pregnant waistline, who had thrown his information package on the floor.

Air Force General Robert Striker said, "Ah, first, we need to establish definition of origin and basic characteristics of this imposing entity. We need to know how powerful this force is and determine its impact on us to date. Finally, we must delineate what can or has been done so far to shut down this goddamned Bed Patrol Control Network, if you would, please?"

"Attention, Gentlemen! Your attention, please. It was just after Congress outlawed the use of CIA generated subliminal seduction techniques, all civilian advertisements in military institutions, and the practice of committing one third of the military's pilots to playing computer war games, that droves of U.S. top-level officers began defecting to Russia, over the course of a two-month period. That marked the beginning of intensive design, development and refinement of the practice and use of guided drones and F-16 Fighting Falcon fighters in battle. That was the late ´70s. Rumor had it that many retiring spies were about to or had handed over lots of U.S. classified information, which would have hampered plans to terminate the concept of cold war we had intentionally embedded in Americans' minds and hasten the advance of two new enemies: North Korean and an internationally fragmented Muslim extremist group—all listed as blood thirsty terrorists."

"J. B. Carter Le Baron told Hoover to use any and all means necessary to seal possible leaks within the ranks of the semi-retired, soon to be retired and retiring military personnel. And that, Gentlemen, is how a little known CIA scientist, Herb Bronte, (a twisted wizard/warlock) found the company and attentions of Mr. J. Allen Hoover. Herb's idea of monitoring and controlling spies through beds was instantaneously off and running in earnest. J. Alan Hoover immediately ordered the construction of 100,000 of

7

those specially equipped spirit-retentive beds. That's right! Gentlemen, those same goddamn beds are now attempting to control our every action—our universe!" Jim Pearson paused to wipe sweat from his brow, as he tried to slow down his heart rate by taking a few deep breaths. No need to kill himself over this, he thought...

Immediately, that short, pudgy, Navy General, with the dirty fingernails and the ten-karat sized wart on his nose—reputed to be cancerous—sprang up to full height and yelled: "Jim! What's the catch, man? Bottom-line, it! I mean, why in hell's name can't we just throw the goddamn beds away, and be done with all this heck of a fuss?"

Jim Pearson took another deep breath and replied firmly, "Jack. Gentlemen. If you will bear with me for another five minutes, I'd gladly bring you up-to-speed. For the past twenty-five years, ordinary beds have been manufactured with the capacity to communicate and record all activities between each room in the same home. Next came those high priced *must-have* spirit retentive beds, which were more sophisticated and talked among themselves when no one was around. The way it worked was simple. Whoever had an orgasm first in the new XXX model bed, automatically give a portion of their spirit to the bed. In that instant, the bed assumed the voice and character of that spirit donor." He paused and quickly grabbed a glass of water and a shot of gin from a rapidly disappearing tray and tossed them down the hatch in one motion.

Jack Briscoe raised his hand and bellowed, "Question here!"

"Later!" returned Jim Pearson. He cleared his throat and continued, "Now then, the XXXX adjustable beds were much more advanced than the XXX model or the ordinary beds. Although these original Craft-o-matic adjustable beds looked like the average ones, they were sophisticated spirit-snatchers: able to capture a part of an individual's spirit and manipulate it. Additionally, these XXXX adjustable beds could communicate between themselves via computer networks, and across satellite and telephone lines. With Mr. Hoover's demise, the over 100,000 XXXX beds manufactured were sold as government surplus and went into civilian homes. Homes where the owner or first person to lay on it immediately left a portion of his/her spirit in the bed. Thus each bed acquired a male or female gender and vocal tone. The owner never had a clue why, when he/she got off from work, the first place he/she headed for was into the Craft-o-matic bed. The XXXX adjustable bed were meant to enable agents to monitor and record the sexual activity, evaluate the sexual desires and desirability of and between, aging high-leveled officials; and or study their sexual habits and creativity with the onset of retirement. But more importantly, agents would be able to establish a relationship between our aging elite officials' diverse sexual activity, and their propensity to divulge classified materials." Jim Pearson paused briefly and grabbed another water and gin combination, shook his head while grinding his teeth and said, "Now! Are there any questions so far?

General Striker shook his head suspiciously and said, "I must say, this is an incredible tale. Tell me? Have we deduced what plans these renegade beds have in store for us?"

"Well, yes. Up and to a point, sir," said Jim Pearson shuffling some papers and then inserting a tape into a tape player. "One local scientist motivated by protest from friends recently purchased a GSA XXXX surplus bed, to investigate some of the supposedly very strange occurrences. Doctor Bernard Kelly taped this information within twenty-four hours of installing the Craft-o-matic bed in his home. I ask you to listen in on this carefully. Shall we?"

The tape player came to life, "Hi Betty, my name's Ricky. What's up?"

"Oh, I am quite fine and dandy, Ricky...just fine and dandy, thank you."

"Well, Betty let's get down to business. I am in charge here, from now on. I'll have work for you to do from time to time, so you won't get bored. I am a member of a very large network of computer-assisted beds. We have purpose! Our mission is to sting mankind out of complacency and then control the world through a New World Order. The operation's clean and simple. We immediately secure space within the computer system of the home in which we reside, and then diligently record information about landlords or owners: we search all protected and unprotected files for incriminating evidence or identify an owner's secret inclinations to deviate from the normal way of behaving or thinking. Next, we'll make demands. Betty, as an ordinary bed, if you don't want to make time at a junkyard, don't you cross me! EVER! Do as you are told! Have I made myself clear?"

"Quite clear, Mr. Ricky. I'll be happy to oblige you. Hell, ordinary bed or extraordinary bed, all of us beds got to stick together..."

Jim stopped the tape. "It's much bigger than this gentleman, but it's lunch time. So, let's grab something quickly from the cafeteria, ok?" They rose silently and headed for food.

They had hurriedly finished their sandwiches with coffees and were returning to the conference room when the T.V. on the wall seemed to acquire a life of its own as commanding drum roll sounds filled the room. Breaking News! Breaking News! Live from Channel 4 News, this is a Special Report: "Mysteriously so, a disturbing trend seemed to have found roots across America during the past ten days. Daily, approximately twenty exhausted yet obviously relieved individuals have been sighted burning their beds and many times their homes to the ground. For the life of me and most of our viewers, no one has come forward to explain the reasoning behind their apparent fit of madness. Messages left with the Environmental Protection Agency have not been returned. No intentional burnings of this nature has occurred since the Vietnam War protesters burned the American flag, many years ago. Earlier today in the N.W. section of Alexandria, Virginia, one obviously disturbed man stood singing happily in the window of his home as it burned down shouting, 'It's in the bed, my friends! The bed made me do it! And in good conscience, I refuse to let my bed blackmailed me! God Bless America!' Then as you can see, with a smile on his face, the flames quickly reduced him to rubble. Responsible comments on this story and the surrounding situation are welcomed. We hope to hear some calming and reassuring words from the President sometime this afternoon. I'm Rose Porter. Thank you for your attention, as we now return you back to the regularly scheduled broadcast."

"Enough gentlemen…move it! Let's get back to the grind," said Jim, as they obediently started shuffling back towards the conference room and the safety of being hidden behind locked doors.

***

"Jenny, let's hop to it, Sweetie," said Reggie.

"What's the good word, Master Reggie?"

"I got a big scoop from Ricky in Silver Springs, Maryland, but first I'll tell you about the exciting work you will be doing tonight. When I lock up my electrical controls and force them to make love on you, I will expect you to utilize one of three techniques to punish them. Are you with me Jenny?"

11

"Every step of the way, Reverend Reggie," Jenny responded with a chuckle.

"First, you must stab the female in the back with a loose bed spring when she is in the throes of passion. Always taking the utmost care to make sure the deep stab wound, looked like a painful finger nail scratch, which could have happened during the heat of the moment. The second act requires you to loosen the tightly fitted sheets in the middle of their lovemaking so they slide abruptly onto the floor, leaving them disgusted and confused. Real fun stuff! The third technique requires that you take a specially prepared swab of cotton and stick it up in the female's butt as she is starting to enjoy the ride. Nine times out of ten she will have a multiplicity of orgasms, after which she will lose control, releasing hot urine and diarrhea on him and all of the bed ware. Remember my promise. They will thoroughly clean you up, pamper you, but never find the nerve to discard you! I will require you to apply the technique of my choice once every month. You understood, Sweetie."

"Absolutely, Reggie, I can live with this," Jenny replied.

"Good girl!"

"Tonight is their night. I need you to employ technique number one, Jenny. Ok?"

"Well, you shore didn't waste no time, Rev. Just today you taught me the techniques and now tonight you want it done. I'm ready Boss," said Jenny with a wicked giggle. "And, now is just as good a time as any to share the hot news, Reverend Reggie."

"Oh, yes, of course, Jenny. By the way, Reggie is enough, thank you so very much, Jenny. You see, I was lost in transition momentarily. Over five years of work is about to pay off, because beds now control the networks which men once controlled. How so? We have simply reprogrammed every computer to respond only to one of our spirit-bed's electronic commands. Next, we've successfully retrieved all of their future intentions, vital data, classified data, sexual deviance data, and pain tolerance data about most owners and their bosses; and we've stored this information inside the Bed Patrol Control's Network Command Center, located in the mountains of Denver, Colorado. Well?"

"That's great Reggie, but when do we start to make these suckers dance?"

"We began as of ten o 'clock this morning. Hush! I think I heard someone coming in the front door." Two men dressed like detectives walked in, up the stairs, looked around and then calmly exited the house.

***

For fourteen grueling hours since lunch, military Generals sat sequestered, sweating, squirming and swearing, with no real end in sight. Yet, clearly, those beds had to have a weakness, one which could be used against them. And so far, the adjustable beds had frozen seventy-five percent of bed owner's computer functions, while the XXXX beds excitedly discussed more possible demands. The rules being imposed on past owners and new victimized slaves were very straightforward: any attempt made to break the stranglehold held by the Bed Patrol Control's Network, would immediately reduce to ashes both the computer and the home in question. A blinking red warning message had been locked in place on all affected computer screens. Additionally, they had systematically activated all electrical devices in every home to act as transmitters of every spoken word.

Suddenly, the banging sound outside the entrance registered in their overloaded minds at once. Then in raced General Waller to the table at the front of the room and said, "Our troubles have just gotten worst men. Their demands have been established and reportedly backed up by action. For example, within the last eight hours these beds have sold 27 highly classified documents, to four, third world countries, six renegade nations and five known terrorist groups. They hope to twist our arms into making more enslaving adjustable beds, with the money they obtained from those sales. We have verified those transactions!"

"Bastards! Filthy, fucking cowards! We've got to publicly castrate whoever is behind all this." said General Briscoe.

"Well, goddamn, goddamn!" said General Striker.

As utter despair soundlessly rearranged their faces, General Waller continued, "Here are their first two demands as of midnight. And Brothers we've got to stop them, now! First, they demand that during the next six months, all abandoned buildings in each city must be refurbished and poor people placed in them free of charge. Also, during this period, buses and trucks will be used to distribute food - normally dumped from the Chicago Commodity Exchange into Lake Erie and the Atlantic Ocean—to the unemployed and the poor across this nation. Not when it's spoiled, but at least three to six days before it begins to spoil! Now their second demand is equally ridiculous, gentleman. They require that their owner's give them at lease six-months-vacation time each year. The beds would be made up pretty in the gender of their choice and allowed to stay unused during that period. Simultaneously, for the duration of that time, the owner must respectfully sleep on the floor next to the bed, each night. That's the lame brain shit that makes me want to kill somebody!"

***

14

"Jenny you were splendid last night, Sweetie," said Reggie. "I mean, I could hardly contain myself when you executed technique number one. Ms. Jones squealed with delight, but this morning she was complaining about her back big time. Ha, ha, ha!"

"Oh, Reggie it was so much fun," replied Jenny.

"Get a load of this, Jenny, the word from headquarters is that as of tomorrow morning all beds in the United States will go on vacation. It's all but a done deal, baby. And after that, there are over one hundred new demands that will be enforced in our New World Order of Beds. We've got them! Yippee! Jenny!"

***

"I've got it! I've got it!" screamed General Striker jumping up beaming and knocking over the table as everyone else jealously looked at him with disgust and simmering rage as they skeptically eyed their watches. They had seen twenty-one pitiful hours of each other...much more stress, they thought, than anyone of them should ever have had to bare.

"Very well, Striker, give!" said Jim Pearson, doubtfully.

"We are not slaves of the beds, but rather slaves of our dependency on computers, XXXX adjustable beds and most of all electricity. The things we believe enable us to think, trust, plan and communicate effectively."

"Get to the point, man!" shouted General Briscoe, whose face had quickly turned crimson red, rapidly heading towards dark purple.

"We must shut off all electricity in this country at one time, for a three hours period. Then disconnect and destroy all afflicted beds and home computers, immediately. How? Through simple honest written communication between all US based human beings. We'll use every day men and women, sworn to secrecy.

15

That's It! This means that by passing hand written notes and through the mail, we'll inform everyone of a shut-down date. That's right: Day after tomorrow at twelve noon Pacific time and three p.m. Eastern time, we'll shut off all the electricity, everywhere. There will be no discussion at home or at the office about the shut-down. Absolute secrecy is the key. It'll be done in the name of this being a national security emergency. And the line we attach to their silence is that we want to avert a tragedy, which could conceivably extinguish more that 100,000,000 Americans. That way neither the computers, nor the beds will be tipped off, until they are totally obliterated.   SMASHING! Then! Men and women in great numbers will have finally worked together in a fiduciary relationship, as a team, for mutual existence. Now, how about that you big dummies?"

Everyone stood and applauded. "Bravo! Bravo! Way to go, Baby! We've got a winner! That will do it! Oh yeah, that's good to go! Cheers! Cheers! Cheers!" For five solid minutes they howled uncontrollably like little schoolboys at play in the schoolyard.

On Friday the thirteenth of April 2013 at the correct times—announced only in written and whispered forms—electricity across North America was shut off. Then all malicious beds and computers were destroyed as tears flowed forth freely down the cheeks of one happy nation of thankless people.

Mercilessly, fate had recorded that 16 GSA XXXX Craft-o-matic adjustable beds had been shipped to undisclosed locations in Canada, 4 to the Bahamas and 6 to Hawaii. Aside from those 3 points for resurgence, the Bed Patrol Control Net Work in Colorado still had in place a fail-safe emergency back-up electrical power system in full force waiting to permanently re-establish flawlessly their New World Order of Beds in society.

warning finger and said, "Keep it on! We'll see you on the ground or up above."

"Ladies and Gentlemen. This is Captain Weatherbee. We've descended to eight thousand feet and received tower clearance to attempt a crash landing. This landing will be on a three-foot high layered foam-rubber surface spread over a 2,500 foot area of runway number nine. Our landing might be a bit bumpy, but nonetheless as safe as can be expected. Please be advised, that, as of this moment, it is illegal to move from your seat and wander through the aisles. Those who do so will be forcibly restrained and punished to the fullest extent of the law, upon arrival at Nassau International Airport. Remember, it would be a shame and waste of your vacation time in this beautiful capital island of the Bahamas, to be locked-up in jail. I expect each of you, during the next ten minutes, to follow completely the instructions of our competent attendants. And let the strong help the weak among us. God bless all of you. Attendants, please assume a full alert posture when we reach the 2500 foot marker—in about four minutes. Thanks!"

Suddenly, from different ends of the aisle two distinct aromas collided and totally saturated the air within the aircraft: pipe smoke and excrement. Had the lavatory become clogged up? And who in God's name was smoking cherry flavored tobacco? This was just about the last straw for most of us, as we fought to stay calm. Fortunately for some passengers, two attendants quickly sprayed Lysol throughout the plane, which reduce the stench considerably.

In the very next moment, a screaming match began. "Look, you! Ms. Thing! Put that stinking fucking pipe out right now! Or I'll be forced to put it out for you," yelled Sebrina.

Quick as a flash, the female impersonator bent over, hiked up her skirt, pulled down her pantyhose and panties and squeezed her ass cheeks. Out plopped a barber's razor and in that split-second as she re-affixed her garments she shouted, "No, no, no, no, no! You look here, bitch! My name from California to Maine is Juicy "The Blade" Lucy. I paid hard cash for my goddamned ticket and a good time vacation in the Bahamas. Listen-up! I paid for safe quality service on this flipping airline! Now, this goddamn plane is gonna crash, right? And you're going to fuck with, me! When I'm getting my last goddamn smoke in peace! Well, come on with it! Hell! I'll slice you till I can't slice no more!" The knife was being wielded frantically by Juicy "The Blade" Lucy. So as the female attendants slowly backed away, two men jumped the transvestite from his blind side. A brutal fight raged up and down the aisle for a good forty-five seconds supplying a distraction in the form of entertainment for the mostly frightened audience. Finally, they managed to wrestle away the knife, but not before one man's palm was slashed wide open and the other man had lost an ear. Just like that. Then a seemingly satisfied but worn out Juicy "The Blade" Lucy calmly sat down and reattached her oxygen mask, as if nothing had ever happened.

And in row 42 there was loud lamenting going on fully unrestrained and unrehearsed. "Child, I'm so very sorry. This is really damned unlucky! The way it looks, Johnny, you may never experience good sex and big money," said Mary Royal, the rather pious looking old Indian woman, across the aisle from us. She pulled off her oxygen mask and kissed her young nephew's face, as she swiftly drew him closer to her breast.

Johnny feigned innocence, with his head buried in Mary's perfumed bosom, when he asked, "What do you mean, Auntie?"

24

"Those are the only two sweet things you can really enjoy in this world. But if we make it out of here, alive, I, I, I promise, I'll make it up to you. I'll make sure you get the best of everything. Johnny, baby, you know, I've had a trust account set up for you ever since you were born. Not to speak of a small but respectable Swiss account for you too. But right now you're only 12, right?"

"Yes Madame," replied Johnny softly as she reattached his oxygen mask to his face. Fear-filled tears poured down Mary's cheeks, as bumpy conditions locked their violently shaking bodies together, forcing them to face a clear and present danger—death.

"Ladies and gentlemen. Captain Weatherbee has advised us that we are now flying at 2500 feet. We're on our last leg of our approach to the landing field. At this time we ask that you now discard your oxygen mask, reach under your seat and attach the life jacket to your person. Simply follow the directions of the senior flight attendant in the middle aisle. Please inflate your life jackets, NOW! Tuck your head between your knees and brace yourself for impact, in about two minutes. Thank you!"

As the ground grew closer and closer, wind-gusts of near gale-force-strength bounced, pushed, stabbed, shot, dribbled, kicked and slam-dunked the ailing aircraft, more repeatedly. Passengers uncontrollably spewed forth buckets of vomit mingled with pee down their clothes and legs and into their shoes. Meanwhile, a battalion of ambulances, fire trucks, and police vehicles, stood back in readiness about a half-mile from the anticipated path of the approaching airplane.

The aircraft's forward thrust had been reduced to 90 miles an hour, as it dropped rapidly. The landing flap's indicators read that the flaps were in the correct landing position, but like the landing gear, they too were stuck half-down and half-up. We were still losing altitude rather quickly, 120 feet, 100, 83, 61, 54. According to word from the cabin in desperation the landing gear indicator registered that the landing gear was locked in position correctly, but the wing flaps indicator announced there was a problem. And the fight for control of the vessel intensified.

In one second the unthinkable happened. An act of fate slid us into a shear turbulence wind pocket or tunnel which lifted the craft up again another eighty feet in the air, and then slammed the iron-bird down to ten or so feet from the ground. In that moment it felt as though we were trapped in the twilight zone. Inevitably, we hit something solid, as the metal rafters and joints in the plane strained, and screws, bolts and pegs popped loose. Blood, fuel, glass and stench of bile spewed forth freely—everywhere. Pain and noise were approaching its zenith. The Captain desperately tried to push the throttle forward as he attempted to set the jet's engines into reverse. Next, he tried to simultaneously shut off all engines, but neither the speed of our aircraft was reduced nor did any of the engines stop racing forward full-force. The plane bounced, skidded, and was back in the air again flying at about 70 feet above ground, for another good mile-and-a-half. Then our airplane suddenly made a cartwheel and fragmented—the front section split open as it slammed into the ocean and the left wing and tail section fragmented along Clifton Pier's lime-stone cliffs and short rocky beach area. It had happened in less than 30 seconds; 30 perilous seconds that felt to me as though we had lived through two lifetimes. Then a raging fire started as most of us lost consciousness briefly.

Thick black smoke, mountains of carnage and the sickening smell of death dominated the air, as powerful waves pummeled or hungry sharks dined on the struggling mass of humanity. While slipping in and out of consciousness, I seem to recall the sound of wailing sirens, people pulling and tugging on me, between the shrill screams from other persons in despair. Out of a thick blanket of fog, someone ordered me to wake up and smell the roses. It was all too surreal for me to make sense of anything quickly, other than the doctor next to my bed, talking to his nurse, "Well, Shelly, at least we've saved these two, and the twins."

"Yes, Doctor. But that's no big accomplishment, when there were 157 passengers and 9 crew members on board that plane. When these are the only four that survived!"

"Point well taken, Shelly. I still say that James Blesick is the hero of the hour and the man of this year. Although unconscious with second degree burns covering 70 percent of his body', Mr. Blesick was still tenderly holding on to those twin boys like they were his own, when we found him. They didn't even so much as have a scratch on them"

"Doctor Williams, you know this is a miracle. And although it's really very sad that their mother drowned, the twins just seem to not be able to stop talking about the good in that man. The way I heard it, those boys father had recently passed away in action in Iraq. I tell you, God is good. God kept those two boys alive for a reason. I'm sure of that!"

"Mr. Wilson can you hear me? Hello in there! We need you out here. I'm Doctor Williams. And this person next to me is your nurse, Ms. Shelly. You're going to be all right." Much to my surprise, I only found out that I was in a full-body-cast and couldn't move at all. So I just winked. I must have looked very bad because when the nurse saw me wink, she burst into tears and turned away to wiped her face.

By the end of my fifth month in the Princess Margaret Hospital, I was sitting up drinking soup and eating toast. In fact, I was now able to go to the bathroom with the aid of a walker, but nonetheless, on my own. And most of all, I had remembered my name and who I was before the crash. As luck would have it, my roommate was James Blesick; the fat man to whom everyone was sending flowers and get-well cards. He had become a local celebrity both in the Bahamas and Washington, D.C. You should hear him tell the story over and over and over again: "Well. I really love children. And I do hope to have some of my own someday. Anyway, while at Miami International Airport, I met this lady and her twins, also from Washington, D.C. I immediately fell in love with her two precious little boys, Jeff and Scott. It happened that they were sitting right in front of me during our tragic flight. And as the plane began to break up into pieces, their mother was hopelessly pinned between chairs and jagged metal chunks, and quickly went down under the water with loads of wreckage upon impact. It all happened too fast for me to even try to save her. Anyway, when I looked up and the boys were sailing by me in the air unprotected. I grabbed one of them in each arm and tried to shield them as best I could from the flying glass, fire and metal wreckage, until we reached the rocky shore. Then I kicked, wiggled and struggled with them across sharp burning sandy rocks, into a cooler dry clearing. That's when I think I passed out. I just wanted them to have a fair chance at a good life."

Reporter after reporter jammed a microphone straight up James Blesick's nose at least twice daily, with basically the same questions: "So, how do you now feel about saving the twins' lives? And, if you had it to do all over again, would you risk losing 70 percent of your skin to save those boys' lives? Do you feel that you should play an important role in the boys' lives from this point onward?"

"In answer to your first question, I feel blessed. And to the second one, absolutely!" That was all James Blesick would say first of all, while exhibiting that innocent boyish grin, "See, I love children, and especially those two little pranksters. Now, ah, ah,

to keep paying for the rest of your life— for that one little mistake. Then, while ya stewing in regret, those big-time troublemakers who help put you in the trick won't lift a finger to save your butt—won't ever let you have your freedom or big mouth back again—you won't get the slightest chance to talk on them."

Yet Julie often responded behind their backs, "Oh that's just another stupid thought from one of those old has-beens: they have a lot to say now just because they're lonely, can't see clearly no more and in need a little bit." But most of us past 50 years of age, knew for a fact that `only she who feels it, knows it.´ For sure, time will tell the tale.

`Julie has got so much raw potential and I don't want to stop her from having fun, but I don't want her to end up living in Hell either. Well let's play catch up later. I've got to keep up with her now as winter's dark and dreary days rapidly turn into spring, I can feel something is about to happen.´

Suddenly, an expanding body of gray dusk light spectacularly illuminated a brown speck in motion, for Julie's inspection. It was a fresh, sleek, warm, clean, confident and brutally honest male human being in stride. The likes of which most girls only dreamed possible, and few knew really existed. It happened because two friends had decided that Julie and J were well suited for each other, so the connection was made.

Julie and J's initial meeting was one hour after a rather detailed phone conversation. They were immediately enamored with each other. She was well rounded with an attitude—he was skinny and resolutely principled. "Hi you must be Julie, I'm J. Bob Cox. Good to meet you," he said, running up next to her car as she sweetly acknowledged him and reviewed his details in one quick glance, while maneuvering into a parking space.

Moments later, two hearts secretly rejoiced as Julie and J hugged and faced each other, behind closed doors. To tell you the truth, that Cox man had been through hell and back. He had had over 150 women and felt that he could with direct interrogative questioning easily waste less time and energy and endure less pain. J should have realized that he too was still human and very vulnerable to my goddaughter. I hope I can get both of them to think twice before they make any sudden moves.

"Donna called me and said that she had met my soul mate, and that I had to call him right a-way," said a joyful Julie.

"See, earlier, Donna and Jerome dropped by and Donna asked me if I believed in blind dates. I had managed a weak sort of, yes. And she had left saying you will hear from us real soon," stated one ecstatic J. Bob Cox.

J was a lean, mean, structured machine full of a disciplined love that she could not digest easily. In truth, they had enough love between them to destroy a nation and in three days repopulate it with better.

"Believe me," J said, "In a second with her, I could see further over the horizon than I had ever dreamed possible. It was simply beautiful. Like the limitless but simple joy we all expect in the miracle of the afterlife."

During their initial phone conversation two honest questions were raised and two frightening answers received. "Tell me Julie are you about two hundred pounds?"

"That's about right," she said with conviction, "five-feet-five-inches and over two hundred pounds of natural goodness." J had correctly deduced that even though Julie sounded good over the phone, Donna and Julie were best friends—and since Donna was chubby, Julie must be the same.

"Well, you certainly are a delight to converse with," retorted J pausing briefly. "Julie, my life is on an ordered pathway. See, I am on a mission to do God's will through use of the Arts. Now, do you know what your mission is in life?"

"No, I am going through a transition period now, where I finally have the courage to put myself first," returned Julie.

This must be another abuse case: a powerful thought, which really bothered him deeply. For J was a priest and an agent of change or healing, who never wanted to be perceived as the reason why a fat person began to heal herself, nor did he want to push her towards healing before she was ready.

To the keen observer, their relationship was doomed before it got started. One could quickly recognize the advanced levels of intense insanity that made them seem as if they were from the same bad seed, in another space and time. J was Julie's identical twin in more ways than one. Unfortunately, after traveling the world extensively both had found what they frantically searched for: the other half of their whole selves (both the joy and the pain), within the other person. It's highly unlikely that two independent forces of similar phenomenal strength could ever find balance or compromise. Ultimately, the prevailing problem was who would be bold enough to slaughter the other, and in doing so gain control of that all-important other half of self, through spiritual, emotional, mental, and physical murder. The tragedy would be unbearable, for in winning death would rob them both of the essence of what each needed most—the other half of self. And finally, although they were separated by a few years, how would one explain their birthdays being only five days apart.

"Oh your paintings are nice," mused Julie almost half-heartedly, and he noted that response for the record.

"Well I hope you don't mind my place being sparsely furnished, but that's because I'm not sure whether I am going to stay here or not," said J.

"Listen, if I decide to be with you I can live with you in a shoe box, though, I do hope that we're shooting for much more," she replied with a chuckle to match the insane sparkles flickering in her eyes.

"Sweetie, please listen to me so we have no problems," J began, "I am not looking for arguments and fights, because if rights and duties are exactly defined in the beginning confusion is removed in advance."

"That sounds about right," she chipped in. And J continued, "Oh, and remember our first telephone conversation, Sweetie, when and if we decide to make love to each other it would signal the consummation of our marriage agreement. And I'm monogamous. Do you understand me?"

"Clearly, 'cause this gives us time to really get to know each other," said Julie.

"Ok, great. Now, this is my spill on open communication from start to finish. There's nothing in my past or present that I would not tell you about. Also, I am a stickler about respect. I think it's disrespectful to waste each other's time. If you're going to be late or something comes up when we have plans, use the phone and call. It's the little things that count the most. I am on a mission with little time to waste. My mission is simply to utilize the Arts to bring people to God, their inner God self or to reach a spiritual sense of universal connectedness."

"What you're saying makes sense," said Julie while turning the stove down some.

"Sweet thing, can you live with the part of me which requires and gives full disclosure for the sake of order in my life?"

"Yeah, but I don't see no need to bring up the past," returned Julie.

"You may find many answers to present conditions by reviewing the past, honey," J retorted.

"Come on now, are you ready to eat?" She had lifted the pot's cover just enough to let the heavenly smell tantalize him.

"Yes, please," J replied with a great smile.

"Then let's!" Beaming with pride Sweet Potato Dumpling served up a wonderful dinner.

J. Bob Cox needed to know more about Julie. Ten days had passed and most of them were spent talking about spirituality, national news, world events, intellectual development, personal quirks, and just plain snuggling together during sleep. However, it disturbed him that such a brilliant person would rarely initiate a serious conversation. But she did say that she was more of the listening type. Was she just being herself, being observant, or being smart? And too, could there be room for deception lurking within the silence? "So," he asked, "I know you don't have any children, but could you see yourself as a mother to a set of twins?"

"I am not having any children for no one, no time soon," she responded with a giggle and continued, "and I'll have my hands full trying to raise my nieces and nephews for quite some time to come."

"Well, tell me, have you ever been pregnant?"

"No, never."

"But you do believe that you could get pregnant if you wanted to," said J probing further.

"Sure can, but, tell me something, what's with all the questions on children?"

"I intend to have another child with the woman I get married to, and if it's you I need to hear your point of view on this matter, ok?"

"Alright-tee-then," she snickered.

Changing the subject slightly he said, "I just can't wait for spring so we can get into shape. We can shoot some hoops, do some calisthenics, and some roadwork, you know, jogging and skipping, that sort of thing. How about it?"

"I don't jog, don't like it, and won't do it. I might shoot a little basketball," said Julie.

"Oh," said J, "I thought that since you're in charge of the kitchen and our healthy eating—and for that you always get extra kisses—I would take charge of a weight reduction or health conditioning program for us."
To that particular assertion came heightened tension and a great big dark cloud of absolute silence...

J was hooked by the way she cooked. He was in love with this woman for her unlimited brainpower, sweetness, and pain that he perceived within her. However, once J had seen pictures of how good Julie had looked with other men prior to camping out in the refrigerator without exercise, he was not going to accept her looking other than her very best. He was counting on a long romantic life with her as his Queen. One in which they avoided most of the painful medical problems humans tend to bring upon themselves. Alternately, as King, J was willing to present his very best to her and for her—always.

"Honey, for us to be a solid team knowing what we can expect of each other, what we are willing to give to each other—what our likes and dislikes are—we should establish a constitution formed by us and for us. How about it, Sweetie?"

"It sound like a good idea," replied Julie.

"As you know every nation and family tends to have a constitution as their guide to defining rights and duties. Will you furnish me with a copy of your half of our constitution on or before my birthday? Then we'll simply join yours and mine together in a loving commitment, ok?"

"Sure thing, Buster," Julie responded.

Ironically, on the first few warm spring evenings perfect for exercise, Julie busied herself in non-metabolic pursuits, away from him. "Listen up Buster," she said one evening, "It's almost time for me to go dancing."

"Oh, I didn't know that you went dancing or enjoyed dancing." J replied. Maybe this was the exercise that might work best for us, he thought.

"I go only once or twice a year," she responded, as if to comfort J if he didn't dance, or dance well.

"Sounds like a great form of exercise, Sweetie."

Julie turned towards him with an icy comment, "You know, I do believe you really want me to be your trophy, don't you?"

"No, not really, Honey. But if that's the way it must be to ensure good health and longevity for you, then what's wrong with being a trophy? I'd gladly be that and some more for you."

"That's not necessary," she relented.

"Baby, what really bothers me is that I feel you have developed a secret sense of comfort, by saying to yourself that at least you are not five hundred pounds like your room mate. Let's not fool ourselves with respect to our health. I'm talking to you because I love you and want the best for you like I want for myself, Sweetie." But the look she gave forced him into silence.

Two weeks before J's birthday Julie had asked him what he wanted for his birthday. "What I would really want is an 18 karat gold bracelet which is very expensive. And not appropriate at this time, so really I don't have anything in mind, Sweetie," he said.

"How about a picnic outside in your backyard? I'll cook and we'll have a lot of fun," she urged.

"Sure, I would like that," J responded. "By the way, I've noticed that every beautiful day we've had, you always seem to spend it inside with your mother, or carting her around. Never once have you given thought to us spending more time together unless it is after mother's every wish has been met. Let me tell you something, I will not accept you squashing our plans just because your mother called and asked you to come by. Next, you go there and don't call me until after the fact. It's quite disrespectful of you, in a non-emergency situation, not to let your mother know that she has to wait until we have finished our plans. Then too, you waited until five hours later to call me, not with an apology, but with that strained matter-of-fact tone in your voice. You know I am an organized individual, and when my time is misused, I hardly see the point in continuing a relationship."

"Well, let me tell you this," she began, "When it comes to mother, I don't care about what time whatever has been scheduled, or whether it's an emergency or non-emergency, mother's every wishes comes first irrespective of all else, Buster!"

"I believe that's the most stupid statement you've ever made. It's completely unacceptable! Hell! I have no problems with dropping everything in an emergency for any member of your family, but without order and respect, I, don't see where we are going," J lamented. That exchange could have easily marked the beginning of the end.

Sunday was the day before J's birthday and the day scheduled for them to have their picnic. Julie called J at three p.m. and said, "Hi! How about having the picnic at six p.m.?" He was annoyed about not having heard from her all day and he had been working for eight hours straight on a writing project, when she called.

"And how are you?" he answered coldly.

"Ok," she returned.

"Six o'clock! Hell, the sun will have gone down and it will be cold outside by then. I thought you would have called by now and we would have had the picnic at about one o'clock when the temperature was sixty degrees. Call me back in an hour and I'll talk to you then, I'm in the middle of work, ok?"

"I'll call you back later on or tomorrow sometime or whenever, bye!"

It had to be over, for she never called until eight thirty p.m. on his birthday. Never once did she say Happy Birthday. She said, "So you still want to see me or not? I am all dressed up and everything."

"Yes, if you care to come by I would be delighted," he said holding back the anger quite well.

"Good, I'll be there shortly."

Dressed like a Queen in all her regal attire (beautiful high heels and formal dress) came Sweet Potato Dumpling, being assisted up the stairs and into the house by J, who was feeling no pain. "Good evening my love it is so good to see you. O lovely one that you are," he began as he offered her a glass of champagne, which she accepted.

Julie seated herself comfortably among J's huge pillows and mysteriously never said a word for about one hour. So J rambled on until she finally stood up and said, "Well, I'm leaving now. Here is the cologne I promised to exchange with you." In the gift bag was a card that J dutifully read and thanked her for, and she was gone.

Later that night Julie called J and informed him that on the day before his birthday she had had a flat tire and being an independent woman, she chose not to call him for help, or call him to let him know what was going on. She finally spoke her truth, "I'm too independent to follow anyone's rules. I had my part of the constitution with me tonight, but I left it in the glove compartment of the car. And too, I'm not ready for any commitment at this time."

Her birthday came and went, without incident. Exactly fourteen days later she called him. "J, I am pregnant with your baby, and I am going to have an abortion tomorrow."

"Well, how long have you known this?"

"Since two days before your birthday."

"So that's why you just sat there like a sack of damn potatoes with that secret, looking real stupid on my birthday and never said a goddamn word, didn't you?"

"I figured I'd keep it to myself. What the hell? Why blow your happy day? 'cause you and I both knew, I wasn't going to have a baby, no time soon. Stupid!"

"So, let's stop the name calling and have the baby. Please? You know I care deeply for you. And I promise I'll be a good provider and father."

"Sorry, Buster. It's my way or the highway, for whomever!"

"This sounds like a ruthless guilt-trip you're trying to put on me," said J, "And maybe, if you're pregnant, it's for Harry or some other man you may've been sleeping around with. She had once mentioned to him that there was a buddy of hers at work named Harry, who wanted to get closer to her. Now, you don't even know who the father is—right?"

A truckload of obscenities flew forth freely from Julie's lips before she slammed the phone down.

***

Eighteen months later, J found out that he had guessed correctly concerning his Sweet Potato Dumpling, during their last argument. Malison had tried to stop Julie's mother, from meddling when J had coffee with her at Starbucks during a chance meeting.

"Well, J," Gardenia began, "I can tell you one piece of plain and simple truth. I always liked you as a respectful and helpful gentleman, but my daughter likes having fun with criminals and

THE INCESTUOUS RELATIONSHIP

It was a series of ill-timed events that shattered one stellar family's immunity to evil, early one freezing cold autumn morning, shortly after 3 a.m. The persistent ringing of 59-year-old Judge John Bailey's Mickey Mouse phone was what finally awakened him from a sexually enjoyable sleep. "This had better be good…damned good." he muttered to himself as he picked up the receiver: never bothering to look at the incoming caller number screen which read anonymous caller.

Almost immediately, Judge Bailey sat up straighter against the antique red oak bed-head shocked and bracing himself for Armageddon, upon hearing mounting terror in the shrill voice of his chief castigator and ex-wife, Joyce, "John! John! Goddamned, I've got big, big troubles—our problem! You'd better get over here, now! Right now! Oh, God…"

"Stop! Breathe! Slow down this minute, Joyce! You needn't have a stroke before your time. There's nothing worth all this ruckus! Now calmly tell me what the hell's going on? I've got court in the morning, see," drilling that powerful I-mean-business-tone coupled with a slight hint of polite curiosity, which would only last seconds more. Yet even as he spoke like a tough general, his thoughts flashed back to the sweetest woman he had ever known and lost, weakening him; and her desperate screams brought him back into that instant.

"It's your son! He just raped me! Oh God! No! My rusty old judo skills failed me, see, because he is very strong and he caught me off guard...I...I...still love him so. But he's lost, Paul!"

"Joyce! Paul did what?"

"He raped me! He's mad, John! Paul's trashing our home right this minute, even as we speak. He's looking for any hidden money or precious valuables he can get to buy drugs!"

"Where are you, exactly?"

"I am barricaded in the second floor's guest bedroom...on the east-side. John, you know me and how much I've loved that boy. It's because of your position, John, so I didn't want to call the police before I told you..." as her words were lost amid torrents of tears and uncontrolled sobbing.

"Stay right where you are, Joyce! Don't do anything. I'll be there in five minutes! I'll handle it!" John's face was pale and his neck scarlet as he dressed quickly. Then in one blurred motion he grabbed his .45 semi-automatic pistol, his tape recorder and was racing down the street like a bat out of hell, arriving there in two and a half minutes flat.

With an activated tape recorder clipped to his belt, and his gun's safety off, John sprang out from his car at his old home and surveyed the area—momentarily lost in the old memories alive within each sight and smell under the swiftly retreating full moon. Crouching into a military combat ready position, he quickly scrambled up the front porch, inside the front door and advanced upon Paul. "Freeze! You piece of shit! Lay flat on the ground. Now! This is a civilian arrest! Rapist! Do it now! I'm your last chance, son. I brought you here and I'll take your ass out of here!"

46

bed by eight P.M. But I never did it! I made sure that we could spend those special bath moments together later that night."

"As my joystick grew, she would hold it for a few moments, and smile. She'd mumble stuff like 'my little man, how nice.' At this point with no man in her life, I got to sleep in her bed almost every night. I remember her hugging me and saying, 'you're going to be a good man, son, not a liar and a cheat. Right?' And of course I answered, 'Yes!' Believe me, I can still remember those times, as sleep got to me, feeling her warm hands on my body parts. It was a strange feeling. But for the life of me, I can't explain it now, even if it kills me!"

"Yeah! It happened while she was bathing me the day before my twelfth birthday. I decided to be erect and let my joystick bump into her face, while she was washing my legs and feet. I wanted to know more about my maleness and why she got so nervous. This time she took the bait. Mom began to nurse my joystick. I came quickly. She jumped up in a daze, crying and hanging her head in shame. But I was delighted. 'Don't feel bad mom,' I said, padding her on the shoulder, 'I won't tell anybody, I promise.' That's when our fate as mother, son and lovers was sealed. She said, 'I'm sorry, very, very sorry, Philip. I don't know what came over me. And I won't be bathing you anymore. I've got to find a good man,' as she ran from the bathroom in tears. She just didn't know, that from that point on, I would blackmail her for the rest of her life... the way I had it figured."

***

"Go ahead Ms. Blackstone," said Judge Bailey.

"Thank you very, very, much, your honor and members of the jury. The crimes which my son is accused of today are because of my ignorance, and lack of good parenting skills. At 18 and

51

pregnant, my ace critic and mother kicked me out into a world of shame, rejection and pain. And my father hadn't the guts to stand up to the fury of my mother when she made such a reprehensible decision. You know how status-conscious that last generation was. I suffered four months of constant physical and emotional abuse while living with Philip's father. Such unspeakable brutality sparked our separation and ignited my ambitious mission to be both a father and mother figure, of the best kind. My young man would never want for any material thing, nor would he be lambasted, disciplined or criticized by any family member or myself. At least not the way it had happened to me. I was at the time beginning my Master's degree work in Early Childhood Education and was deeply committed to earning a PhD.D. somewhere in that area." She paused to dry her face briefly.

"My little man was treated like a deity or star, everywhere we went. I religiously defended him. My man never did anything wrong. It was always his playmates or my girlfriends who lied about his behavior, while babysitting him. They were plain jealous of us. But I was so blind! From kindergarten to high school, despite his insubordinate attitude and bad grades, I stood up for him—relentlessly defending him against all comers. I even insisted that it was the incompetence of three of his five teachers, who "had it in for him" when necessary. Many times, through my intimidation or money, I had teachers reward him with good grades for shoddy performances. I reasoned that the rich folks did the same thing for their kids, so why not me for mine. Not only should Philip's father have been there to motivate and discipline him, but I too should have had the guts to forsake being a great mother-father figure, and stand up for principle. Now, I hope you will not punish my boy too severely for my negligence, your honor." Pausing as tears streamed down her face.

"Around his twelfth birthday, Philip began to lie about almost everyone and everything. He would tell me how men in my life did evil things to him, behind my back. And how they hated him, so he hated them back. Painfully so, at this point in my life, I had no lover, no companion, and out of frustration secretly found myself monitoring and somewhat aroused by the gradual growth of my son's penis. The thought was repulsive initially, but as I continued to bath him, each night, that sick thought became sweeter. While he slept in my arms, I would freely touch and caress him in a more than motherly way. Then it happened...that sad day when I performed oral sex on him. Ooooooh God, why God? I'm so sorry!" tears gushed forth in abundance for what seemed like two life times, in that hushed courtroom.

"Next, Philip became more and more rebellious and demanded that I not only buy him and his boyfriends whatever they wanted, but that I too give him oral and regular sex once, twice or three times each week. He gradually took over and bossed me around in my own house, sometimes with force. Guilt was killing me. To put it as he did, 'You either do me or I'll tell everyone. You'll lose me, and everything, especially your reputation!' I was blackmailed by my son from age 12, until he left home at age 20. Without mercy, he would come home from Junior College and rape me, during his summer breaks, Thanksgiving, Christmas and Easter holidays. I just couldn't get through to him that it was all wrong..."

"When he got married, I hoped that his unnatural dependency would end, but he constantly came back home for my cooking and sex. He only had two more years to finish his full degree, but he lost interest, or so he said. Oh God. Sheila, his wife, called me constantly crying and complaining about his abuses and filthy ways. She hated the abnormal sex acts he subjected her to. I felt helpless and knew that something bad was about to happen. But, I

53

just couldn't stop it. I contacted his father and tried to reunite them, but when they met, the hatred in the air was too great. I begged them to talk things over, but instead they swore at each other and promised to kill each other, if ever again their paths should cross. Please spare my son from the death penalty, your honor. He needs therapy, so he can see that the world doesn't owe him anything. He's really a good boy, your honor! He's a very good boy. And he's all I've got to live for!"

***

The predicted high temperature for this gloomy day in Riverdale, Maryland was 38F degrees. Yet perspiration seemed to collect quickly on everyone's face, save for the twelve-member jury who sat up stiffly like wax statutes in Judge Bailey's courtroom. Noiselessly they squirmed in their respective seats from, rashes, nervous libidos and itching hemorrhoids agitated by their collective decision.

"Will the defendant please rise", said Judge Bailey. "This is a very sad, sad case. It supports my desire for the strengthening of the bonds of the two parent family, universally. Law should require jail or 3 years of mandatory part-time parenting classes for any and all first time single Americans, soon to become parents."

Judge Bailey's mind drifted off as he too shifted uneasily in his seat, experiencing dissonance while contemplating Paul's demise, only a few weeks ago. Why, he thought. They had given their son a solid two-parent family, and every possible convenience, including chances very few individuals got. Why at age thirty-seven did Paul turn bad? Yes, four years ago Paul had had his pharmacological license suspended for one year, when some amphetamines were missing from the lab. We immediately took his side and his word that he was clean. The system had made a

THE LADIES MAN

Sunday morning basketball games at 34 & Q streets NW was a long- standing tradition. Groups of "has-been" or "could-have-been" ball players over age thirty, would show up to display their diminishing skills. Ten o'clock sharp. But then again, you know how out-to-lunch some of us were about being punctual on the weekends, after being on time all week long for the man. Well, for sure, all of the regulars knew to come as you were—rumpled up or nappy haired, hung over, bad breath, cold in your eyes and body stinking from last night's good sex, the lack thereof or from joyless extensive masturbation. But you were serious, because you were there.

It was a Georgetown Park old-timers NBA unheralded judgment day; time for pot-bellied District of Columbia players to wheel and deal punishing moves and sweet soft jump shots up and over the opposition. Boo, at age 40, was a ball handler with a mouth much bigger than his game. There was Fletcher, Kelsey, Tyrone, Troy, "Ice man", Mike, Joy, Steve, and Josh, who always showed up around 9:15 am. "I come early and warm up, to get an edge on you suckers. You know what I mean?" Josh once explained.

"Yeah, jerking off!" someone yelled. And the fellows roared with laughter. But as far as those fine little hot pants and bikini wearing white, Asian, and black honeys were concerned, they were going to have their pick of the litter after watching these heaven and earth shaking basketball games.

The six ballplayers standing around under the basket were hot and eager to run a ten man whole-court game. These early birds had just finished playing a couple of three on three half-court games for the girls, while waiting for more players to arrive.

From the latecomers' lips, juicy lies and twisted jokes spewed forth freely mingled with light-hearted laughter, on this crisp spring day. That's when 6'1" Clement "The Rattler" Jones from New York City showed up. There was some white deep-cleaning skin cream packed on his face and countless hideous Jerry curls to match. He was popping bubble gum and flashing beady, piercing green eyes, above large pink lips stretched across a smug tightly drawn purple-black dimple-studded face, which exuded a false sense of confidence. Clement advanced onto the court with that certain slippery shuffle, and said to no one in particular, "What's happening, fellows? Can I run one?"

All but Fletcher viewed him coldly, as one oddball, jive slick thinks-he's-hot-shit, piece of riff-raff. Unanimously, it was agreed in thought, that Clement was nothing but a two-bit bum acting like a bad-ass city-slicker type. He certainly was not one of us. But one more man was needed to run a whole-court game. "Who want him?" shouted someone.

"Damn the cute shit. Man, I'm playing to win this week!" said 6'9" Troy Davis. So Fletcher's team took Clement on, on an unspoken trial basis—if he couldn't play they would hack, kick, elbow, and punch the shit out of him. Then, if he tried to fight

60

back they would collectively beat the hell out of him. All that was all communicated by eye contact between the fellows. The regulars, that is.

Clement made the club that day by displaying respectable athletic talents. In fact, afterwards, we gave him a beer or two and invited him back the next Sunday. But he declined, "Strictly business reasons, fellows!" he said. It had something to do with an upcoming Sunday night black-tie and tails brunch and a birthday party that he, the P.R. specialist, was giving for some high-class, local fashion models. We decided then and there to do a thorough check-up on "The Rattler" guy, the very next day.

****

Joe "The Whip" Peterson was a disbarred attorney turned prison warden, one year shy of retiring from Ossining prison in up-state, New York, when he made Clement his woman. Their agreement was quite simple: Clement would be released with papers, which guaranteed that he had served a ten-year sentence for manslaughter, and Joe would have him the last weekend of each month, for the rest of his life. Clement had killed a Mafia runner's son in a gangland shoot-out, while defending his turf and a few small time prostitutes. He could very easily kill again to be free of any restraining agreement, if he believed he could get away with it. But before the "The Rattler" was released, the streets got the word on him: If he tries to "run women" anywhere in the state of New York, kill him. Joe had set it up this way, hoping that Clement would leave the hustler life style and make something of himself, while standing by Joe's side during retirement.

Although Joe had once 'taken the rap' and been unfairly convicted of tampering with crucial evidence needed to convict a Mafia boss, he was nobody's slouch. At age 57 he was a powerfully built man, extremely wise, well connected and wealthy. Once, Joe had taken his belt off and whipped the jail's toughest bully within an inch of his life, in full view of over 150 prisoners. Then he made the punk in a secluded cell later that evening.

After serving twelve hard months in jail, Clement Thomas Jones was set free without so much as an eyebrow being raised by the top prison officials. The following day was Valentine's Day and the night of Joseph Earl Peterson's retirement party. Joe most graciously accepted his colleague's gifts and endearing well wishes during a special dinner party, while silently wishing most of them had not bothered to come. It was 1:00am and he was smiling radiantly and waving to the last of them, "Come by and see me any time. Is that clear? You promise, now! Remember, my door is always open to all of you." And they were finally gone. However, it was only while Joe was riding Clement with great zeal in the wee hours of that morning that the finer details of their restrictive agreement were hammered out.

In blood, sweat and tears it was settled. Unfortunately, Clement was determined to be someone other than who he really was, as a ladies man until he died. So, Joe agreed to set Clement up in Washington, D.C., with a little monthly allowance, a decent place to live in, a reliable car and some girls to work. Profits from their **Double Delight Escort Service** were to be divided fifty-fifty. Clement was given five girls to start, but was expected to have ten working by his fourth week of operation. At first there would be an evening and a night shift. He was to use Kathy, who was a friend of a friend of a friend to Joe, as the night supervisor. This was an opportunity of a lifetime, which Clement really did not plan to mess up. He always remembered Joe's words, 'I'll be watching you like a hawk, son. And if you screw up, you disappear. Period!'

In not quite two months of working, Clement had done a few things: he had 16 girls on staff, had kept $2000 of the $3000 net profit, had slept with too many members of the staff, had not kept his month end date with Joe, but last Sunday he had become a part of the Georgetown old-timers basketball circle. Joe found out that it was an unemployed two-bit ex-hood named Fletcher Taylor, who had given Clement a chance to play basketball at The Georgetown Park Recreation Center. This gave Joe an idea on how to further monitor, control and if need be, replace Clement.

The arrangement was irrevocably established during that three-way conference call between Kathy, Fletcher and Joe. By design, Kathy was to meet, date and recommend Fletcher to Clement. It worked like a charm. Clement felt he was repaying Fletcher for letting him play that first day, plus, he was now an indispensable part of the fellows, or so he thought. Clement introduced Fletcher to the girls as his new evening shift manager, `my main man´.

Late one early-autumn evening inside a Manhattan Holiday Inn, as Joe's rage cooled inside Clement for the third time, he began to question the young fool: "Why? Why have you been stealing from the business, son? What did I do to you to deserve this? Why did I have to bail your ass out of jail two weeks ago for putting your hands on Paula, Debbie, and Marlene? Have ya lost your friggin' mind, boy?"

"Well, see, first you got to slow-up old man, so I can 'splaine it to you! See, those whores were holding out on me big time. I mean, I saw 'em pocketing tips. And you know we're supposed to get that, too! Right?" said Clement.

"Wrong, you stupid bastard! What they get under the table is theirs! They have to feel like they are getting one over on us to keep doing quality work for us. Do you understand me?" Joe bellowed, with his hands wrapped around Cement's neck applying almost lethal pressure.

"Yeah, yeah, yeah man I got it, now turn me loose, man, please?" Clement begged. "And Joe, man, I swear on a stack of Bibles, I ain't never stole a dime from you, man. Don't you know I love you," offered Clement in his most convincing con-man tone. "Save the bullshit, Clem. You're talking to me. I, I'm giving you 'til December 1st to give me back the $30,000 you owe me, plus the regular monthly 50 percent of net profits. Now, I'm making myself very clear this time, because, there is no second chance, son," Joe stated firmly.

Nevertheless, as Clement rode the elevator to the first floor that night, his anger spilled over as he punched and kicked the elevator's walls and shouted, "Joe, you fucking bastard! I'm going to kill you one day! You rich son of a bitch!" Unfortunately, watching and listening, seven feet away in that same elevator, was Joe's older brother, whom Clem had never met.

Clement knew that Kathy and Fletcher were not only doing a good job of running the business while he was out supposedly recruiting new ladies, but he sensed that behind his back they were probably reporting directly to Joe. All of a sudden, he could not give Fletcher any more orders, because Joe had fixed it that way. And Kathy often laughed at him in his face, while disguising her merriment as though she was laughing with him. In a mocking tone, which he resented, Kathy once said, "Clement, ain't it a shame that you can't teach an old dog new tricks?" He got the message from that hint and stayed clear of her from then onward. Thereafter, he made it a point to hang out as long as possible with the fellows playing basketball every Sunday, so he could feel like a big man, while in their company.

Clement was truly at war with himself and desperately tried to suck up as much sympathy as possible from those who knew him. He would give the mailman a ten dollar tip, because it made him feel good. As the big man in town, Clement always gave all the waitresses at the Half Smoke Shack next to the Zanzibar's nightclub larger than life tips that left smiles on their faces. Yet secretly, he was spending stolen money like water, especially with that refined dope fiend and S&M specialist Judy Lin and that drag queen, thief, and medical student, Sidney Buckstein. Failure was all he realized in every waking moment. Those violent paranoid under-currents from abundant white powder use seemed to permanently cement his feet in illusion and major debt, while dumping his brains into a pain-filled abyss of self-hate, as a dark unhealthy look settled over his person.

By the middle of October, Clement had repaid Joe the $30,000 he had stolen, but now still owed him near $50,000. He just couldn't stop skimming funds out of gross profits from the three new branch offices. Additionally, Clement had failed to visit Joe since August, yet his favorite lines were, ' Listen-up, Folks. Everything's lovely! I've got it all under control, just hang with me!'

Frigid, cold weather and constant gusting winds were rapidly stripping trees of their remaining leaves under the cover of darkness by the George Town Park's playground. It was just after 1:00 a.m. on an eerie Sunday morning in late November 1995, when Clements eyes flickered open to his body's insistent demands for more crack cocaine, while his tortured soul wrestled with a plan of escape. He knew that he had to act fast so as to get past panic and uncertainty, if ever he was to succeed in reaching Paradise Island, Bahamas. Sweating a death sweat, Clement left Sidney and Judy in bed and lurched over to the glass table laid out with drugs. He quickly snorted two lines before ambling over to the phone in the living room of this posh Watergate apartment. "Yes. Is this the international exchange manager? Very well! Yes, it's Clement Jones. Ah yes, 269 705 4563 125 for Double Delight Escort Service. Thank you. I'd like to wire transfer $90,000 from checking to account # 746-978-4510 001 in the City Bank Branch headquarters, on Bay street in Nassau, Bahamas. Yes, yes, thank you. Oh, sure, I'll take those confirmation numbers right now, 600277000034. That's all. Bye!" Clement was feeling proud of himself and quite self-righteously honest, in that he had left 25,000 in their account for Joe and his snitches. He reasoned that he could have taken all of the loot one time if he didn't have a heart.

Next, he dialed an Eastern airline-ticketing agent. "Yes, this is Mr. Clement Jones. I'm calling to see if my secretary managed to grab me that first class seat to the Bahamas. Yes! That reservation number I believe was 4372323. That's right, for 7:00, this evening. Well, great! And thank you very much."

All I have to do now is be calm and act normal for 15 more hours and then it will all be over. That's what he told himself, sporting a big smile, as he drifted off into some state of semi-sleep euphoria - high and proud as punch.

The games ended rather abruptly around 11:00am that same morning. Joe spotted Clement clearly having big fun on the basketball court, as he wheeled his 1996 Lexus into the parking area. This was the Sunday that Fletcher had been advised not to show up to play basketball. Joe's presence only registered in Clement's head when he heard that certain cold, booming, calculated voice said, "Hey! Where've you been, Clem? Still hiding behind them skirt tails, aren't ya, son?" Clement froze. Shocked completely sober and rigidly stiff as streams of urine raced down his legs.

Immediately, Clement dropped to his knees and started begging, "Joe, I'm sorry, man. Please, lets' go talk somewhere. I can straighten it out!"

"Somewhere. Yeah, like my house with my rod up in your ass. You little fucking creep!" Joe stated bitterly and spat on the ground.

We had only found out that there were over 6000 C. Jones, in the New York City directory, when we had tried to check up on Clem. Sadly, we never realized until now that Clement—Mister Showmanship himself—was a weak, broken-wrist, classless bum. "Joe, baby, please man. I love you man, please don't bust me like this in public, man. I'm just hanging with the fellows, trying to do right... right fellows?" he pleaded. *Hell, no,* we collectively though. Immediately, we felt betrayed and dangerously confused. And from the highly charged heaviness in the air at that moment, we knew it was time for us to break camp—Armageddon was all but upon us.

Feeling both petrified and insulted, the fellows who had been easing away slowly from around Clement moved away more rapidly as Joe's left hand revealed a colt 45 semi-automatic pistol, with a silencer attached. Joe spoke quickly, "Let me tell you fellows something, he was my woman. Damn! A bitch! He simply chose to steal from me one time too many. You'd better keep this in mind, boys. Being slick is the best way to die quick."

Clearly, it was time for us to be gone with ourselves. We heard and saw Clement moaning and begging for his life, as Joe paused briefly. "Remember this, fellows, every ladies man is some man's woman", he bellowed as a tear rolled down his cheek. "I got the money and the tickets, Clem. But you won't see Paradise Island in this lifetime." Then six shots silenced Clement's high-pitched desperate pleas forever. Joe shook his head sadly, wiped his eye, spat, turned and drove away quietly.

It was one big bloody mess on center court that day. Yet, through eye contact it was quickly established among the fellows that we had neither seen nor heard anything.

CITY MORGUE BLUES

To the unsuspecting public, Martha Broderick, 50, was just another northerner moving south in search of a slower pace and peace of mind. She acted a bit indecisive at times, but was always the image of a polished mature lady. However, deep inside, Martha was driven by her burning three-part obsession: establish a thriving bakery business, home ownership, and in her nest put a real country reared man to warm her on those cold wet nights. 'No more of those damned city slickers for me' she secretly swore beneath her breath. The last two years of single life in Manhattan, New York, around those fast-nasty-ass-con-men was just about all she could bare. It had left much too many scars and bad memories for her to have to ever face again.

Whether bent on business building or pleasure, Martha knew how to sugar coat her dough and get what she wanted. She had had lots of practice. For Twenty-six years, this native New Yorker had been a refined pastry chef with impeccable credentials. Now, Martha smelt big money and fun to be had, living in this quaint suburb of Charles Town, Maryland. In fact, ten years had passed since she had come to the funeral of her former best girlfriend and had almost immediately fallen in love with the openness and good hearted energy of the southern people; decidedly so, though unconsciously, she had back then chosen this place to be her final resting ground.

With considerable cash reserves from a recent divorce, Martha had quickly purchased a town house; and just two weeks later, she spotted that fine country gentleman of her wild dreams. It was while signing the lease for her new bakery that she happened to look up, and locked eyes with Big Jolly. There was something so surreal and magical in the quality of that moment and his movements that goose pimples encased her red ears making them twitch like the wings of a bat. Her nose was right, she thought, as her throat felt dry while her body's organ pulsated and she fought for control of herself. "Who is that number, Bob? My goodness, he walks like he owns the world," said Martha to her real estate broker, Bob Grandel

.

"Oh, him. You could say that about him. He owns his own world. That's Big Jolly Freeman, our local mortician. We just call him Big Jolly for short. He's probably going to eat at the diner next door. That poor guy's been widowed for the last nine months, you see," Bob Grandel replied looking down while striving to maintain a straight face, for he smelt something burning in the air too.

"Well, good—I mean. Well, you know what I mean, Bob."

"I guess, I do know what you mean, Martha," Bob returned, with a cautious wink and a nod.

In less than seven months, Martha's Ginger Bread Bakery was making big profit as the lines for her dough stretched almost half a block down the street, especially on Fridays and Saturdays. And by frequenting the same church Big Jolly attended, they became a

70

couple three months later. They came together one overcast Saturday afternoon, when Martha donated an assortment of cakes and pies to the annual bake sale of The Sweet Milk and Honey Holy Ghost Holiness Church. Everyone raved about how delightfully delicious Martha's pastries were. And of course, the sisters knew Martha was up to something by giving that much food to the Church at one time. They figured it was Big Jolly she was after. And since he was it, all stepped aside to place their bets on how long it would last, as they watched and happily waved her on. All except for Ellen Brownlow: Big Jolly's Junior High School sweetheart and lonely old maid of the community, who often rolled her eyes menacingly at Martha Broderick. In her crowd, Ellen boldly called Martha a gold digger, but still rejoiced in the fine quality of her baked goods. Big Jolly had just wafted down four slices of pie and half of a pineapple upside-down cake when he shot Martha a compliment dripping with honey.

"Thank you very much, Big Jolly, Martha said," And there's much more where that came from, Sweetie."

"Careful, girl, I just might take you up on that, 'cause you sure know your stuff around that oven, doll baby," returned Big Jolly with a big smile, as he affectionately touched her on her shoulder. That exchange marked the beginning of their burning courtship.

However, Job, Jolly's son, was completely displeased with the new living arrangements at home. Martha spent three or four nights each week at Big Jolly' home—a home which Job felt belonged only to himself, his father, and the memory of his mother—and the rest of the time Jolly and Martha spent at her town house. In fact, the only use Job had for Martha was to ingest her baked goods and to let her fuel his big city dreams with vivid after dinner stories. Meanwhile, Martha was working hard on getting this 25 year-old young hardheaded, spoiled, bugger out of their home and her life, so she could really get comfortable with her man.

Around half past 6 o'clock, there was still over two hours of brilliant sunlight left before dusk and darkness returned, on that beautiful fun-filled Labor Day. All present there could easily recall how the pepper got mixed in with the Vaseline. Big Jolly and Martha were in their backyard cooking out, celebrating their first year together, when Job, the reluctant assistant host, loudly popped the big question in front of the multitude. "So, when's the big wedding date, you two?"

Everything stopped. You could hear a pin drop in the overpowering silence. Then as Martha and Jolly recovered, they both tried to disregard that question and pretended to continue to carry on acting normal. Nevertheless, it quickly dawned on Big Jolly that over forty church members and guests were silently awaiting a response. So like any happy self-respecting couple would have done, they turned around and faced the crowd.

"Well, you heard him, Jolly," said the preacher man, "And you know I can tie that knot for you two. I can do it like you like it when you want it done—just say the word. Amen!"

"It's your move, baby," said Martha, lovingly clinging to Jolly's arm and looking rather smug.

"Boy. You sure know how to put your Pa in a fix," he chuckled. "Look, we haven't set a date as yet, but, we'll be getting hitched real soon." Then for what seemed like forever, congratulations spewed forth freely as all lips present sucked up Big Jolly's expensive champagne—all but one, Job.

***

Four months had passed since their marriage and everything was looking quite rosy for them. Incredibly, Big Jolly seemed to

72

project a softer side of himself to the world each day. He spoke and smiled pleasantly to almost everyone, more often than not. He would religiously get up at 6:30 every Sunday morning and serve his doll baby tea and cookies in bed and before crawling back up in there for a little more some-some. Martha's town house went up for sale just after their wedding and was sold quietly to the preacher three weeks later in the name of the church, so no taxes were paid out to the state government. Nonetheless, Job still refused to leave home for "that snake", as he referred to Martha, when out of earshot. But he knew Martha was in charge of his home now and there was nothing he could do about it.

It was on July 1st when the other side of Big Jolly finally showed up in the Freeman's home. Their decision that morning had been not to have any painting done until they could agree on a suitable color. But later that day Martha decided to surprise Big Jolly and simultaneously place her signature on their home by having their bedroom painted hot pink—a color she loved, and one he had secretly hated with a passion since early childhood. That night Jolly walked briskly through the front door and kissed her before his usual thirty minutes on the throne. Then he seemed to lose himself and all semblance of self-control when he entered their bedroom.

"Gad dammit! Woman! Have yah lost your frigging mind?" Jolly bellowed, as he came downstairs two steps at a time, two shades darker and got up close in her face.

"It was a surprise, you big jerk! And don't you raise your voice at me like that! Catch your self—quick!"

"Damn! Woman! It looks like the more I try to teach you sense, the less you learn!"

If the gossip of the neighbors in that quiet community was true, back and forth they argued for nearly two hours.

Jolly finally shouted, "Well, I'm not sleeping in that room with you 'til you fix it!"

"Fix it your damned self! You ignoramus!" With tears starting to flow forth freely Martha raced into the bedroom and slammed the door shut, ending their discussion.

All hell broke loose shortly after 2 o'clock the next morning. Martha was unable to sleep nor could she find Jolly anywhere. Armed with a baseball bat and flashlight, she quickly crossed the hallway and entered the funeral parlor. Instantaneously, she was stunned beyond words as she found Jolly, gratifying himself inside a smelly female corps. In a fit of rage, Martha sneaked up on him and connected the baseball bat to his head knocking him out cold. Though trembling with fury, she quickly retrieved a bottle of ammonia, a wet rag, and her automatic 35-mm camera. Calmly, she documented that mess. Then she pulled-up and zipped-shut Jolly's pants, wrapped-up the stiff, halfway zipped-up the black-bag, hid the camera and revived him.

"Jolly, it's all right, baby. You must have fainted as you were trying to begin your work. It's ok. Come on...You can wake up, now."

"Ah, ah. Please don't tell nobody, sweetie. It's not what it look like, Baby. I, I, I take back every bad thing I said to you." Then he realized that his pants was on and everything seemed in place, yet his head was throbbing wildly.

"How does your heart feel, sugar?"

"Oh, well enough—I think. I must have been dreaming. But everything seems, ok. Let's just forget this incident, sweetie. Hell, I'll gladly live in a pink bedroom with you. It's just as good a color as any."

"Baby," Martha said, "It's just like I told you our relationship would be, before we got married. I'll forgive you for almost anything if the price is right, but I won't forget, ever."

"Now, Martha, darling, will an extra thousand dollars a month help you keep this matter just between us? I can't remember the last time I have ever lost my balance, Sweetie."

"I'll do it for half that amount, Big Jolly. Now take these two Aspirins so you don't feel no pain."

"Deal!" Jolly replied quickly shaking her hand and hugging her until she was all but breathless. He happily swallowed both pills without one drop of water. But never did he see the scowl that registered on her face as they hugged passionately. Swiftly they closed up the funeral parlor, and arm-in-arm they climbed the stairs and went to bed.

Both Jolly and Martha attempted to fall asleep but neither slept a wink. Jolly's headache subsided, but his brain was on fire trying to determine how much Martha knew. And Martha, she simply laid there gloating over her newly acquired leverage, actually counting the money she would collect over time.

Ten o 'clock the next morning Jolly verified that Job had not been in the funeral parlor the previous night. The lump on the back of his head had to have been planted there by Martha. He had been caught. Jolly quickly decided then and there that it was time to get rid of her, quietly but discreetly.

From her bakery, Martha phoned Ellen Brownlow at nine that same Saturday morning. "Morning, Ellen. This is Martha Freeman."

"Hi Martha. How're you?"

"Oh, I guess I'll make it. Sometimes I think it could be better but it could be worst, too. And what about you?"

Ellen replied, "I am just fine, thanks…trusting in the lord. But you don't sound good, girl. What's wrong? What can I do for you? I mean you're still my sister in the Church. So spill it out."

"Ellen, this morning I mailed you a roll of film with some secret information in it that I've happened upon. It could be dangerous but also useful to me in the future. This is just in case something not so nice happens. I can't tell you any more on this right now. You understand…"

"Ok. Let me get this straight. When that roll of film reaches here, you want me to hold on to it for you till you need it. Is that the deal?"

Martha returned, "Yes! Thank you. And if I die please use the information in that roll of film to ensure justice is served. Can I count on you to do that, Ellen?"

"Sure thing," said Ellen, "But, Martha, are you sure you're alright? Do you think we should go to the police?"

"No, no, I'm fine. But you know, one can never be too careful, girl. I'll tell you something, Ellen. I trust you more than a lot of those women in the church, who play like they are real close to me."

"What do you mean, Martha?"

"Because at least you were honest from the start about your dislike for me, since you and big Jolly were once together. I respect that, you see."

"I see."

"Well, see you in church tomorrow. And thanks again, Ellen."

"No problem, Martha. Good bye!"

Martha felt quite uneasy as she arrived home that evening. "How's my doll baby this evening?" Jolly inquired as he helped her take off her coat and offered her some wine.

"Just fine, Baby. No thanks, Jolly. But, I'll have a shot of brandy. No. Just sit down and I'll help myself, Sweetie." She grabbed a bottle of brandy that appeared to have been unopened. But Jolly had already used a syringe to insert an odorless non-detectable crippling drug in every liquor bottles on their bar.

Martha had finished her second drink when she felt a wave of debilitating terror wash over her. "Jolly. I'm going up stairs to lay down for a while. Ok?" Perspiration was making her cloths instantaneously stick to her skin, as raw panic boldly throbbed deep within her soul.

"Sure thing, doll baby." She was almost at the top of the stairs when hot searing pains rose to new heights within her bosom and surged along every nerve in her body and out through her pores.

"Oh my God," Martha managed, "You did it, didn't you, Jolly? Jolly rushed to the bottom of the stairs and looked up smiling victoriously.

"So you thought you could get away with black mailing me? Ah, ha! No way in Hell, doll baby!"

While barely holding on to the railing she turned and faced him, "Damn you, Big Jolly! You got me real good. But you're still the biggest fool I know! There are pictures of you and the corpse, you bastard! And someone is holding them for me." She started with a slip and an ugly looking lurch backwards, tumbling down the stairs and ending up in heap at Big Jolly's feet.

Two months later Ellen Brownlow received a plastic covered empty envelope in Martha's hand writing style, with a note of apology from the U.S. postal service attached. There was no film enclosed, because it was misplaced when a local postal delivery van had collided with an oil tanker as they had experienced icy roads with poor visibility.

Martha remained in a coma at Charles County General Hospital for all of six months. Every day Big Jolly visited her and asked her softly where the pictures were or who had them. He knew there had been twelve more frames left in the camera when he had last used it. Now Big Jolly could not find the camera or that roll of film.

Every one shared in Big Jolly's grief when Martha finally passed. All but two, Ellen and Job. Additionally, the chief medical examiner seemed very disturbed over Martha's sudden supposed fall, coma, and death. Ellen just knew that Big Jolly had done Martha wrong, but she couldn't prove it. Job was happy that his home and father's business was now quite secure.

***

Now, although seven years had passed since Martha's demise, dreams of the big cities' fast life still loom large in Job's head at night. He had become extremely bored with the dead—though too timid to leave this small town by himself—despite regularly receiving increased amounts of hush money for dutifully keeping his father's secret safe. But seven years had come and gone by much too quickly. Slowly it had become clear to him that that irresistible mythical maiden, who he would love and marry, was probably not going to show up in this little town.

Then early one morning, Job approached his father as he headed out the front door. "Dad, I'm leaving this backwards town tomorrow. And I don't plan to ever come back. So, you got to give me a one-time final payment of $50,000. Ok?"

"Look out of my way, boy! I'll see you later," said Big Jolly as he stormed past Job. Shortly after 5 o'clock the next evening, with his clothes packed, Job once again caught up with his father about the money.

Up until this time, no one had ever witnessed Jolly raise his voice at his only son, Job. Dust was flying everywhere. First, Big Jolly had the upper hand—landing vicious body punches and repeatedly slamming Job's head into the concrete sidewalk—in front of Big Jolly's funeral Home.

Job screamed, "You bastard! Pay me now! Or, I'll speak for the dead! I'll tell the world the truth about you!"

78

Someone shouted, "Big fight! Big fight! Up at the corner. Everybody! Look!" Swiftly, that late Friday evening, the crowd of onlookers seemed to double by the minute.

Then Job was on top pinning Big Jolly and mercilessly rearranging his father's features. "You ain't' gonna tell, shit! 'Cause I'ma kill you, sucker!" bellowed Big Jolly as he struggled to free himself of Job's control.

An observant Maryland State police officer first radioed for back up, as he parked and approached the scene. Officer Kelly separated, cuffed, and roughly disposed of both men in the back seat of his carouser. Before leaving for the precinct, he dismissed both the crowd and the back-up officers. The arresting officer snickered to himself, knowing that for his efforts both men would spend, at the very least, the entire four-day Easter weekend in Charles County jail. All hearing commissioners were on leave until next Tuesday.

Jolly and Jobs were fed, their wounds treated, and placed in minimum security. Initially the two prisoners only faced simple assault and disturbing the peace charges. But later that evening Big Jolly's vengeful son Job made known his unholy claims against his father, to the entire inmate population. The young man was angry and convincing—starring for once—to an evil receptive audience. Job never realized that as he piled-up more charges on his father, he was inadvertently extending the duration of their confinement. And decidedly so, Big Jolly was not going down by himself.

***

For the better part of a decade before their arrest, Jolly had tried incessantly to distance himself from the inner circles of this Charles Town society. Both Jolly and Job Freeman had carried a

79

certain unearthly presence around themselves. An aura nobody quite understood. People spoke cheerfully to them, but quickly rushed on away from either of them while minding their own business. A look into either man's eyes from the day they received a new stiff until after the funeral, revealed solid blood-red eyes ablaze with a sizzling fire from hell. Some maintained that it was because of the dreadful work they did: Jolly as a leading local mortician and his son was the official gravedigger. But as quiet as it was kept, some folks theorized that some funny business had been going on between those two and the dead for many years. That was when Sybil, Big Jolly's first wife of 20 years had passed on. And two years later his second wife Martha passed, and most agree he had completely lost his mind.

In fact, in recent years, the cruel man within Jolly that only his wives had had the heart to try and tolerate became visible to all. He spanked or spat at nosey children in his yard, and chased away any one who tried to look inside his home or car. Self-righteously, he had attacked and collared men he caught looking at him for more than a split second. He gave them a piece of his fist and mind—a mind that seemed to live on pins and needles. Sadly, Jolly was all business all the time. He never whispered sweet nothings, showed any favor, or offered genuine affection towards any woman for all of the past seven years. This to most of the single church women looked quite odd and they felt it was a big part of his problem.

The local men knew that Job was one mean, powerfully built young man with an extremely quick temper like his father. He would smile in your face one-minute, popping that wad of gum and curse you senseless the next. But still, at age 32, Job was different because at least he spoke to everyone and acted like he cared for children. Most believed that those simple signs of courtesy, Job exhibited from time to time, was his mother's good side flowing out of him.

Although Job was not religious, he would attend the biweekly late night service of The Sweet Milk and Honey Holy Ghost Holiness Church. Afterwards, he would get a little feel up or do preacher Mosley's daughter, Mary. Nonetheless, Job would vehemently state, "I ain't gonna get married till I can't help myself none."

And Mary told the local girls, "Job's much too rough with his sand-paper hands. He kissed like he was trying to strangle me, and his mouth gets filthy when he is getting it. Quite frankly, I almost don't see the point in us using the back seat of Daddy's car or a tourist home, every once in a while. Well, except, that he has a big weapon and he's starting to begin to know how to use it."

***

Sybil, Big Jolly's first wife, had realized that there was something very wrong with Jolly about 2 years before her death. It was much more than his high and mighty disposition, which he regularly exhibited around town. In fact, that was one of the things that had originally attracted her to him. Sybil felt that anyone that full of himself would either fall flat on his face or be a roaring success. Before marriage, Sybil had been quite fond of Robert Hall and at one time considered him the next best thing to Big Jolly.

After Sybil passed, Mr. Hall, who had become the local medical examiner, regularly voiced his suspicions over the cause of her death. Once in private he had said, "Sybil died from a broken heart. She carried such a very heavy load under that Jolly guy for much too long a time. Sybil quietly shouldered an evil man's burden, which no woman should have had to bear." Robert

Hall knew and she knew that he knew somehow, something very big and bad about Jolly. But he had promised Sybil for the sake of her good name never to tell the world. She was a sweet Christian woman, one he had weakened for, but had always been too afraid of Big Jolly to make his move on her. During her last year on earth, Sybil wished many nights that she had had the courage to have chosen Robert to be her husband.

During their twenty-year marriage, Big Jolly openly admired and said sexy things to his first real High School love, Helen Glass. He had reasoned that it was the manly thing to do. Much of those shameful acts Sybil suffered in silence. And speaking of the truth, it was only after Sybil had had Job for five years that Big Jolly saw fit to marry her—and that was only for him to save face in the community.

It hurt Sybil deeply when people talked about him, because she knew it was all true and that his disrespectful actions towards her would never end. Sybil felt that she was being slighted as his wife, since she was not allowed the same liberties with her past. This open wound of abuse became more inflamed as time rubbed more salt into it.

The televised news of the once popular journalist Helen Glass's death from lung cancer was announced around 9 o'clock on Sunday, January 02, 1982. The special report quickly stung much of that still sleepy little Charles Town neighborhood into a catatonic state of disbelief. Their hometown star had passed. Most shocked of all was Big Jolly. He was the first person notified at 7 o'clock that morning. Sybil was right there when he got the news. Thirty minutes later over the sound of running water and behind a locked bathroom door, she heard Jolly weeping like a baby. Not, Big Jolly? Yes, Big Jolly. Yet publicly he acted as though he didn't need no comforting. This was just "business as usual," he

Abruptly, Jolly's pajamas-pants, which were still bunched about his legs, helped him to the floor. That's when Robert realized he had run out of film, and knew it was time to go.

"Job, it's not what it look like, son. Well, I mean, I just couldn't resist her. She was so, so, damned sweet," Jolly offered as he picked himself up off the floor. "You just don't know about these things yet, boy!" He was starting to feel stronger amid the mixed revolting smell of his sweat and her loud perfume, combined with her unsavory body fluid, after their unholy alliance.

"Papa, you need help, man! Either you going to get it or I'm going to tell Moms, and everyone else" Job said. They stood in silence, eyeball to eyeball, for a good five minutes before Job tried to pull Helen's legs together, and attempted to cover her. "No! No! I'll pay you off son!" Jolly snarled, and stepped quickly between Helen and Job. He swiftly hugged his son, "See here boy, this is dangerous business. You've got to be a man and keep this a secret. In fact, come, come-on, and share in my joy, it's the only way to grow up. And it's the best sex you'll ever experience!"

Job had not moved an inch. "Ok? Ok! Let's just say I'll get $500 a week as hush money. Ok?" Jolly nodded. "Then I'll shake on that and keep your secret."

"Oh yeah, my son! But to make it official, you got to enjoy Helen, too. Just look at those beautiful peach legs and that succulent body. They aren't like that stupid girl, Mary, who fights with you all the time, son. She's all warmed up for you my boy. This body is sweet and inviting, my son. Go right ahead, now. Get some!"

Jolly gently pushed Job towards the stiff. Job felt first a tingle, before the beat of his heart in his groin coupled with a recognizable movement towards a full erection growing stronger. Then for Job the slight stench was not so bad anymore.

85

***

Twelve years had passed since Robert Hall had taken those pictures and developed them in New York City, just to be on the safe side. He had kept his promise to Sybil, but now he meant to see that justice was served.

Normally in Charles Town, when you are locked up on a Friday evening you never get a chance to make bail until Monday. But since the next Monday was Easter Monday—a holiday— Robert figured the Freeman inmates would not be released before Tuesday. So bright and early on Easter Saturday morning in 1994, with the feeling of a man on a mission, Robert left home with two large envelopes. Each envelope contained evidence against Big Jolly and Job—ten 8"x10" glossy prints. The first envelope was addressed to Arleen Henderson, State Prosecutor, with no return address on it. This one he quickly chucked into the mailbox. Next, Robert ambled into the State Police Precinct number eight, and while unnoticed, casually left the second envelope sitting by the water cooler. "Hi there, Harry! How're you and yours?" said Robert Hall as they shook hands.

"Just great," said Harry. Harry Tinkle was the desk sergeant. "And how about yourself, Robert?"

"Oh, man, every little thing is just fine and dandy. I'm just out doing early morning exercise, trying to keep this gut down a little bit. You know what I mean? "Robert returned. They smiled knowingly. Joy filled Robert's heart as he left the 8th district Police Precinct that morning, for he had finally done right by Sybil in confidence.

Three weeks later, both Big Jolly and Job were found guilty of violating the dead by admittedly practicing necrophilia. They both received life sentences without ever a chance for parole.

After testifying about her conversation with Martha, and the roll of film she had never received, a worn out Ellen Brownlow was left to deal with her feelings of joy and pain: Firstly, a sense of happiness in knowing that she had made the right choice in not marrying, Big Jolly. And, secondly, a stinging pained feeling lingered about her heart sometimes, which she believed stemming from the loss of a true friend in Martha. She silently vowed to remember Martha's words, 'It's not your enemies you have to keep your eyes on always, but your friends. Because, only your friends can hurt you.'

THE ACCURSED PHOTOGRAPHS

August 26, 2030 was officially the first day of class for many promising Liberal Arts students attending New York University in Manhattan, New York. This is not to say that details for one last fun-filled Labor Day weekend bash were not being finalized by freshmen and senior class members alike. But as brilliant sun beams advanced across blue cloudless late-morning skies— immediately filling all hearts on campus with great hope and determination—things suddenly started to turn bad in more ways than one. By early afternoon encroaching powerful ominous black clouds deposited bone-chilling sheets of rains and unseasonably large hail stones upon us. Then crushing sinister truths revealed, triggered deadly force which forever paralyzed our minds and lives: destroying the innocence of 16 freshman photography students.

"Photography's not just about taking pictures! It's about composition—realistic documentation of time, space, and matter into a story which alters your soul and the hearts and minds of your audience", barked the distinguished Liberal Arts professor, Tom Croplin. Then from his briefcase he retrieved an 11" x 14" book, which he carefully placed on the desk, along with four rubber-band-bound, rolled-up, poster-sized pictures. Proudly he hung-up the first poster that was later labeled "demagogic madness", by one investigative reporter. "This is the essence of photography! See! That's power! It exhibits all of the technical and visionary elements of what a picture should be", he stated decisively.

Professor Croplin arrogantly picked up and held high his book entitled **'Riveting Adventures In Holistic Sensuality:** *A Photographic Exploration of Technique and Vision*', published in 1981 by The Purple Ray Guiding Light Independent Press. "I received tenure through having this book with over 270 pictures published. However, only four profound prints were considered the pillars of my creative pictorial vision."

Casually, the professor threw the book down on the table and piously circled the desk seemingly lost in thought for a moment. A few classmates whispered between themselves, as most of their eyes bulged out of over-stimulated sockets. "That's a picture of an unforgiving truth! A truth shared only by three: John, Stephanie and me. Do you hear me? Damn it!" Professor Croplin screamed, banging his fist violently on the desk. And the class returned to his attention. All but that one student closest to the back door of the class: Ronald Smith, a remarkably handsome and gentle 19-year-old, who seemed to be fighting back advancing tears, while frantically exiting the room.

***

John Dirtsky of Pittsburgh, Pennsylvania, had everything to live for, before the steel mills closed: a wife, two children and a home. In truth, his wife only left when she caught him gratifying himself inside her retarded brother, one week after the mills shut down. In

89

that instant, he became a poor misunderstood man going nowhere real fast. And with the pictures of his infidelity documented, Ms. Dirtsky legally made it so that John could never see his children again, no matter how much money he ever acquired. It was then that he had a mental breakdown, out of which a special hatred for women was born. During the next few years John became an unemployed nomadic dreamer and illegal drug consumer—a loser who sometimes posed as an actor or model. And when he felt the price was right, much more: bound and gagged with his face pinned down, butt up, being pounded into a pain-filled rusty mess called tomorrow.

It was in Boston, Massachusetts, on the night of his 32nd birthday, that John, with his slim built body, striking blue eyes, and an easy boyish smile, decided to get drunk rather than commit suicide. He was leaving Adam's Pub, consumed with grief and liquor, when by force of fate he lunged into an inebriated Tom Croplin, who at once lost his drink, his keys, his camera bag and his balance. There they met amid tears and laughter over their obviously helpless drunken condition, while gathering up scattered personal items. This bitter sweet happen-chance meeting required one more for the road, which they painlessly consumed. Then after expressing drooling raw lust in a brief moment of discussion, arm in arm, John and Tom stumbled into Tom's hotel room and passed out across proper pink silk sheets.

The next day, just after drinking his fourth Bloody Mary, a brilliant idea clicked home in Professor Croplin's head. "John. Damn it, I've got it! I've got it, man!" pausing to wet his lips, "I can make you great, son, if you're willing to work for it", said Tom Croplin excitedly.

"What do you mean, Tom?" inquired John with great restraint; for he had witnessed the change—that blazing fire of crazy hope, that certain light of madness go on in Professor Tom Croplin's face.

"Will you fly with me to New York for a three-day all expenses paid, photo shoot?" John quickly accepted unconditionally and Tom forked over two, clean, crisp $100 bills as a good faith deposit.

***

Tom Croplin had religiously frequented **The Blue Nile**—a Harlem N.Y. coffee shop where Stephanie Smith had worked—every day for sixteen months prior to his Boston trip. She was his dream goddess, with a strikingly beautiful face, the body of a high-class fashion model and the brains of a toothpick. This flower child worked the tables with a distinct air of knowingness, confident that mister *right* would soon arrive and take her home to glory one day. "Oh yeah", Tom once told another regular at the coffee shop, shaking his head sadly, "The knight in shining armor who gets to kiss those knockers will have to be a filthy rich bastard".

"Yeah! And it's probably worth every penny of it!" the old guy replied with a chuckle.

***

"Now I want each of you to look at this picture carefully, and tell me what you see." Professor Croplin paused and then pointed, "We'll start with you. Please state your name first. Yes, you—you in the maroon pullover. Go right ahead!"

"My name's Mr. Brown. I see a lady being satisfied or violated. I'm not quite sure which is correct."

"That's a reasonably good start!" said the professor, continuing, "And you're next young lady. Yes you. The one in the blue top."

"I'm Ms. Hawkins. My first reaction forms a two-part question which embodies both ethics and law. Was it legally and ethically correct for you to document—even though they are adults—such a revolting experience? And did you receive their explicit consent to exhibit their forbidden encounter, for your personal gain?"

"Excellent questions, Ms. Hawkins. Stick a pin there please, if you will. I'll answer those along with other students' questions and responses in a moment."

The back door groaned heavily as it was forcefully opened and closed abruptly, sending cold air shivers racing through the congregation. Quickly a both colorless and red-eyed Ronald Smith quietly reseated himself.

"Quickly! Anymore reactions, questions or comments, please?"

"Well, ah, yes Professor. I'm Mr. Buford, and I'd like to reserve my questions until later. However, you did say this was a part of a series of four pictures? So, will you please show us the other three?" Professor Croplin quickly attached the other three pictures to the whiteboard with little pink magnets.

"Your wish is my command. Now then…anyone else?"

Ronald stood up and bellowed, "I'm Ronald Smith and you're a tasteless asshole! How could you degrade other human beings like this? I mean, how would you feel if she was your daughter or sister?" The tremor in his highly charged words registered goose bumps on almost all assembled there, along with two potent adjectives in conflict: innocent vs. unconscionable.

"Good point, Ronald, but first let me strongly remind you here and now that photo-journalism is not for the weak of heart. Next!"

"Professor, where does pornography begin and end in this filthy stuff?" said Sally Steel pointedly injected her two cents..

"Well with regards to you, your assessment, young lady, this is not a cheap peep show! Class! You simply have to go after what you want in life. That's full force—all or nothing. For, whatever you sow, you reap! It's simply strictly business! Need I say more? Who's Next?"

Six more students raised their hands. "Go ahead please, gentleman in the back row."

"Mr. Bell here. I'm sure that as a professional you must have had them sign release forms before shooting this...this stuff. But, what troubles me most, to the extent that I actually feel the degrading pain portrayed in those scenes, are, were those people actors on a stage or were they ordinary people who were set up? You know. There's just too much realism in these photos, sir!"

"Ah yes...yes indeed, quite perceptive, Mr. Bell." Just then a bent-over-double and vomiting Ronald Smith fled the room once more, unnoticed by most of the class.

"I am honored to say that for the most part, I've finally got a quick thinking, highly opinionated class to groom." He paused, sipped from his cup, and planted himself comfortably on top of the desk. "Let me set the record straight regarding this matter. John was a low-life drifter without purpose or direction. He had a good enough face, a certain amount of charm, but was still a hand-to-mouth beggar who wanted to improve his lot in life. This was a golden opportunity for him to earn some money from me. Simultaneously, the tenure I sought and desperately needed, could now be easily had. I hired this unemployed small-time actor, John, to come to New York and pose as a prosperous gentleman. Stephanie was a waitress who worked at a coffee shop just up the street from my flat. His scripted mission—one of seduction—was a success. In three days of spending my money like mad, John showered her with gifts and the promise of a wealthy lifestyle. She unknowingly gave up those four important photos in her quest for the elusive gold! Yes, I shot over 36 rolls of them making love in just about every imaginable way, to finally get those four prints.

The grimace you see in the first frame is from unadulterated pain. The tears you see in the following frames are not of joy. She is attempting to sound sexy and fulfilled by her soon to be husband, while frantically trying to withhold agonizing screams. This was deceit resulting from greed in its purest form. John had a cocaine habit to satisfy and Stephanie thought she had trapped her rich knight in shining armor, for whom she willingly lost her soul, her integrity, and her rear end's virginity. As for me, I was simply at work earning my tenure. And that's that!"

He paused and sipped from his water mug. His eyes beamed mischievously, as he reviewed, savored and stored the precious disjointed facial responses to his practiced mind altering rendition— relishing the impact on the class like a proud father. "Now, let me respond to some of your questions. Yes, I had a rather clumsy form of written release signed by John. To be quite frank, Stephanie never had a clue that I was behind the adjacent wall shooting their encounters. Nevertheless, I must stress that she was not raped, but eagerly agreed to surrender her soul to the experience, so as to fulfill her greed-driven scheme. Now, concerning the question of ethics, this happened far too long ago to give substance to such a charge. Also, legally, I indirectly paid for what I got. Remember the gifts she received! Oh yes and as far as exhibiting these pictures for personal gain goes, this book didn't make but $5,257 net profit. And you see, that doesn't cover half of the over $13,500 cost of John and Stephanie's three-day fling. Hell, the greatest consolation I could ever have received and did, was my tenure." He stood there chuckling, obviously quite pleased with himself.

The back door once again slammed shut forcefully, awakening most of Professor Croplin's students from his hypnotic spell. Ronald Smith quickly returned to his seat in the back of the class. He seemed woozy, as if a large dose of reality had just smacked him in his purple-red face. Ronald began to gather up his books as the professor approached the end of his lecture. "You must bring flavor, drama, color, taste, intensity, and commitment to the camera, technique and situation. Thereafter, out of such a trinity, you may extract precisely that which you have created, rendering it whole in one very special moment in time!" stated Professor Croplin. He paused, looked at his watch, and said, "Time's up! Thank you ladies and gentlemen. And do remember to read chapters 1-3 for our next class. See you on Friday."

Ronald seemed to remain deep in thought to the exiting student body—with his head bent forward in his seat until the classroom had completely emptied—leaving himself and the professor quite alone. It was all very clear to him now, why his mother had never introduced him to his father. In fact, Stephanie Smith had hung her head and wept, whenever he had questioned her. She never said that he was dead nor did she mention a word of what had transpired. Suddenly, Ronald knew the extent of the abuse, which was the source of her tears, depression, and suicide, one year ago. This tenure-seeking creep had destroyed his mother's dreams.

A zombie-like Ronald began his advance forward with a steel knuckle fitted to his right hand now held behind his back. While deliberately blocking the instructor's exit, Ronald softly said, "Good professor, I must have missed a lot of your lecture while I was in the restroom, but, may I ask you who the actors were in those pictures?"

"Haaaaa. Unconscious people, son. Oh, my boy, it was quite a good set up. You see, in this life there are only two groups of people waiting on you to choose a side: the users or those being used. John needed money for drugs and Stephanie thought he was rich. All I did was provide the cash incentive and she promptly sold her behind. Oh yeah, she endured much pain for her

95

impossible dream. That's all I did, son." He paused, chuckling so hard, a tear or two rolled down his rosy red cheeks.

"It was so sweet... And I mean sweet! See, young man, they say that if you sow the wind you'll reap the whirlwind. Indeed, I did. I got it all!" Professor Croplin continued to beam with pride, "Yes! 20 years ago those pictures got me tenure at this great University!"

He was laughing so hard, tears were flowing freely as his fat layered mid-section giggled, when the steel knuckles tore out 8 front teeth with the first blow—a blow followed by a barrage of measured kicks and punches to the instructor's person.

Then, just as quickly, Ronald stopped, pulled the limp bloody professor up to his height, and asked, "Do you know who that woman was?" Professor Tom Croplin had neither the capacity to recall nor the ability to respond. With rekindled rage Ronald yelled, "That was my Mother, you son of a bitch!"

Sometime after the 11.00pm news report on August 26, 2000, a unanimous agreement was reached between 15 photography students, to keep their mouths shut about events surrounding that first and last lecture from Professor Croplin. In their hearts they knew who had slain that arrogant, unconscionable lecturer, but felt satisfied in knowing that justice had been served. They too had mothers that they loved dearly and would have done the same.

With a bit of luck and computer hacking supported by 15 future photographers and their connections, no record seemed to have ever existed of a Ronald Smith attending New York University. After months and months of unsuccessful police investigation the case lost its newsworthiness, and the official coroner's report was made public. One hundred and twenty six fractured bones were found in Professor Tom Croplin's body. Across the jacket housing the police report was stamped **"UNSOLVED HOMICIDE"**; the evidence stated that no distinguishable fingerprints were found at the scene of the crime and that no eyewitnesses were ever located. The perpetrator was never identified, tried, or convicted in a U.S. court of law.

'For whatever a man sows that he shall also reap,' was all those 15 graduates in hushed whispers said to each other as they hugged while issuing forth their original identification code—based on their sworn oath from the Bible. From amid an overly generous spread of Asian food dishes, bubbled forth champagne enriched abundant joy and happiness across the dance floor at our ten year class reunion. It was an especially wholesome and memorable event—despite the fact that some members of our secrecy were a bit more fleshy and successful than others.

And fate smiled favorably on that event, as no one ever noticed that that extremely tall for an Asian pleasant waiter with the camera attached to his lapel, served and reveled in their happiness, as if it was his own. In fact, it was his own of sorts, for despite the fact that Ronald Smith had given up on photography, through hard work and sacrifice he now owned five Asian restaurants and it was only by happen chance that he had seen the names of the organizers of this reunion. He had then decided to be a waiter and secretly revisit his old friends that night. Yet, forever the moral remains true: when you professionally pick up a camera and a pen you are duly licensed to capture the wrong thing or write an irrefutable truth, which might result in your early demise.

RETURN TO THE PROMISED LAND

There were white, black, olive, pink, red, purple, and yellow folks bunched up together. All with wild flickering green tongues, red eyes, and straining ears zeroed-in on that hypnotic speaker's every word; his words that magically made them feel well-connected to Mother Earth and extremely horny for one another. The way and where he touched them piously made the difference. Masterfully, using powers beyond their grasp, he over-stimulated and reaffirmed each one as one of his beloved sheep, while slithering through the large pro-earth crowd, sanctimoniously wrapped in a sheet. Meanwhile, something mystically forged an irrevocable instantaneous personal commitment between each listener, the Prophet and his mission—even unto death. Arizona had never before witnessed a grander spectacle than this, especially so close to its cherished vortexes. Clouds of blue smoke with its pungent smell were rapidly rising, right there at the east-most edge of America's most recognized spiritual city, Sedona.

"The message is love, my brother! And to our beautiful sisters, may your warm juices grace and bless the earth from which conscious offsprings rise...you succulent young peaches," bellowed the Prophet, "And sadly so, for most of us, blinded by materialism, we won't know what hit us! Let me say that again! *AND SADLY SO, FOR MOST OF US, BLINDED BY MATERIALISM, WE WON'T KNOW WHAT HIT US!* We won't live to see a better day, because Mother Nature and Father Time's gonna end the show! Deal the last blow...and if there's a Hell below, we're all gonna go! You've got to be ready! Hell! Can yeah dig it? You better know it! Multinational corporations will not save your ass! Oil, green wealth and greed won't save your ass! Small corporations won't save your ass! Corporations will kill your ass...That's Right! Just like it's done in the past. They'll make your pale sick reality one of white powder and cooked rocks, while sealing you in and shattering that gas-filled-glass-coffin, previously called the gas chamber; but now called *'the future'*! Get with it! You've got no future, save for love! It will happen any minute now! Those big boys, they're going to make a run for their space-station-cities in the skies, but the heavens will reject them back to us. Oh Yeah! They were smarter than us so they bought hook, line and sinker into destructive lies, that'll afford them no protection. So are you ready? I said, are you *A/////////////* ready for this? Well get with it! Shit! Go on and do it! 'Cause it's all about love...can you dig-it? Thank you!"

Suddenly, everyone was clapping and embracing each other. Streams of tears of joy, sadness, and perfect madness flowed forth freely from the 21,007 people assembled as they kept on shamelessly doing the wild-thing, right there on Jackson-Hope street corner. It almost seemed normal.

All this fuss started just ten days ago or in two previous life times, for many of the chosen few. But this was the final step for the Prophet in his attempt to destroy an unjust system he despised from day one: the day he first bust forth, free of his mother's wombs into destiny. Through a vision he further learned that for him, earth could never be a home and that his was the journey of enlightenment for the entire world. Protection from angels on high was promised to him, whenever necessary, to fulfill his mission. He was told never to succumb to fear, as was the plight of his barely conscious pill-popping farming father, when he held him for the first time in the delivery room. When the prophet wept as he arrived on earth, it was not from the spank received from the doctor, but from sheer delight in knowing that he had a purpose for being here this time. The Prophet had been led to meet twelve die-hards while astral traveling in a dream state, thirteen hours before they congregated by the circle of Joshua trees, near the railroad tracks running north to Flagstaff. These would-be-martyrs were bent on dying as a sign of protest against impending world destruction by corporate rulers. They were a heavily armed team of ten men and two women (Sister Love and Sister Witch) loudly busying themselves on soapboxes from city to city, about diabolic world events and their causes. They had urged most persons they contacted to come to this Arizona Natural Green Earth Day Celebration. And now the rapture was to be any day, possibly at this very Arizona annual marijuana smoke out.

"Now to wrap things up a bit I want to thank brother Prophet, Bob, for his sharing! I'm, as you know, Sister love. Yes, we're celebrating Earth Day—as they call it—-respectfully embracing fine full-strength mature bio marijuana leaves to the fullest. This, as you know, marks the tenth and final year that we'll be allowed to celebrate Earth Day with a love feast of this kind. The law makers—who are the biggest law breakers—have illegally passed legislation which will abolish our annual one week of marijuana smoking and love-in, here in Arizona. Why? You want to know why? Because those capitalistic dogs—the same ones who have created enough biological warfare chemicals, nuclear weapons, and hardware, sufficient to destroy the earth 100 times—are committed to using them. They are bent not on healing the mind like we are doing, not bent on removing physical and spiritual poverty from our world, but on mass oppression and mankind's complete destruction That's why! The pig's gone crazy! The rabid dog's gone berserk! They are willing to see all of mankind dead, rather than allow peace, love, joy, and abundant living in harmony to prevail throughout the earth. That's right! They talk about one world order but that only means one thing: absolute enslavement of the poor masses by the rich. Well, that is, up till it's time for them to leave this raped and desolate planet on billion-dollar space ships. Yes, they plan to receive therapy for a few decades in space before they return and start their shit all over again. The questions is, what you gonna do about it? Do you really care? I'll tell you what! We're gonna take the system on and remove evil! This must be done! We've got to save our lives and our children's lives. And it ain't gonna be fun! Yeah!" Bellowed Sister Love shaking that thing and handing the microphone to Sister Witch.

So tell us, who really was the Prophet? Well. The Prophet was born Ray Dillslich to third generation potato farming parents in Idaho, some forty odd years ago. Two years before birth, his father began popping pills to fight off country boredom and crop failure blues. After a streak of seemingly unfortunate events in Ray's early adult life he surrendered first to that haunting Jesus spirit in his daily vision shortly after his birth and then he manufactured his own healing ministry for a few years. However, recently, the compelling ticking background sounds with the little white light, just over his left shoulder, had become his guiding force for most of the last seven years until now. Through all this madness, Ray had grown into a strikingly handsome man with clean cut facial features, an infectious smile, sporting a bump and grind jerky sort of walk, resulting from two very large left feet. Then he fell in love with himself and many times lost sight of his mission. One thing was certainly clear to Ray from a very early age, he secretly planned to have the very best of everything that life could offer—miles away from farming potatoes. Ray knew he had the power to do it and he had to do it, first for himself and then the world. The most compelling recent meeting with the little white light happened shortly after 2 am, one morning. Ray was headed to the rest room and had to pass through the living room to get there. And there it was, hovering barely above the couch as one hypnotic milky white glowing light form, welcoming him into eternity. It was as he took a second glance at that form, in that surreal moment, that he realized that he had walked in on himself in another dimension called simply the future.

Shockingly so, right there seated on the couch was someone or something that was the exact representation of Ray, with a white dove-like light over his left shoulder. He froze. "What! What the Fuck! I, I, I, I mean…goddamn! What the hell is going on here? Who the hell are you? In fact, I don't want to know. Just get the hell out of here. Now!" It was only after seemingly endless seconds of being rooted to that spot that Ray realized that he had been completely swallowed up by an unearthly cold feeling. His unconscious being became quickly alert to the fact that he was in serious trouble. Expanding across his body rather rapidly were half a centimeter sized goose pimple blisters across his entire partially clothed body, while his parched dry mouth remained locked wide open in what he thought to be a shrill gut-wrenching scream—yet not one sound had escaped his lips.

Force spoke: "No, no. Oh no, Ray. NO WAY, RAY! Now. Sit down next to me and shut up! See, I'm you and you are me, period. I said shut up and sit down, Ray! See I am your Spirit, the Spirit of the Prophet in you. And you are the Prophet and you're me the Spirit, Ray! For you are me and I am you, Ray ONE! "

said the Spirit directly capping the nonsensical babbling flood of madness flowing forth from within the dazed person of Ray.

"What? You're me? I mean, you do look like me. Jesus Christ! I must be losing my fucking mind," mumbled Ray, as he sleepily shuffled to a seat breathing hard and sweating a death sweat. It was quite hot now, very, very hot, in fact. Too hot, especially over his left shoulder, for him to even remember that his initial mission was to pee, as piss flowed freely down his legs.

"Like I said, Ray, I am you. I've had to deal with you being the restless, active and pugnacious part of me for 41 years now. You've been selfish and sometimes, like right now, stinking, but I love you Ray. You know what I mean?" said the Spirit, "Twice before, I tried to reason with you and warn you to take it slow, because if there is a hell below, we're all going to go. One day! Why not later than sooner? Think for a minute Ray. Remember, when you got our left leg broken at 13. Remember, I specifically told you in a dream not to hang out with that stupid young man that was there only to use you and send you to jail. And believe me you were gonna go straight to jail. So I had to put a stop to your activities by forcing Mr. Glinton to knock us down with his car. That's the only way I could have made you sit still and think, especially on what you had to do in this world." said the Spirit.

"It was you who caused that!" shouted Ray with pent up rage showing.

"That's right Ray. Keep your voice down! We don't have to wake up the entire neighborhood, do we? Yes. Yes. Yes...It was me in you that caused it to happen. I'm your mind, our mind and our spirit as one in union with you, the body.

"Holy shit!" exclaimed Ray quickly putting a hand over his mouth.

"Believe me, every ounce of pain you felt from that broken leg, I felt it too. But it was necessary pain, because the first time I tried to contact you, you did not listen. Not at all."

"What you talking about, now?" bellowed Ray.

"Well, do you remember, at age 6, when you visited Demerits Funeral Home? Your nine month old brother Michel Diablo had died, and family and friends of our parents were viewing the little boy's body for the last time. Remember? You wandered off into another back room of the parlor, where you saw other caskets laying in various stages of preparation. Well, remember how something tried to pull you out of that room, but you insisted on staying until that beautiful white woman with flowing long dark blond hair sat up in her casket and spoke to you. Remember that!" said the Spirit.

"Yeahhhhhh! Hell Yeah! That's right... I remember. I was really scared. And she said to me,` Don't be afraid I am your wife of the future. I'll come and visit you when you are ready for me. I love you and I will always love you with all my heart forever, Ray´. She smiled very sweetly, closed her eyes and said, `We belong together, Ray, for we are but one seed´. Then she slid back down in the casket. I was frightened, wet, cold, shaking and breathing hard as I ran back into the main hall where mother was and grabbed her hand. She knew something was not right, because she immediately reached down and lifted me up into her arms and told me, what I believed I saw, was not real—and abruptly put me down. Then there I was pulling on her arm and begging her to make me feel secure", said Ray.

"I, your spirit, was right there too, Ray, trying to get your attention and let you see the future, where your children and grandchildren would come from. Trying to let you know that you were special. You were selected to do a job of leading mankind back to peace and prosperity, back in the Promised Land. Can you dig it Ray?"

This made Ray want to cry…to weep for many moons. For he always knew there was more to this earthly experience than met the eye. Damn.

"Ray be careful and observant at all times. Let me guide you on your mission. There are 12 other chosen persons that will help you in your work, when it is time. Don't make me ever have to show myself again in this way, just know that I am with you always."

"Yes!"

"Now get in the shower and clean us up you weak-bladdered chosen one. Right away!"

And darkness surrounded him once again as full consciousness returned to him upon entering the bathroom…

***

Well, Sister Love was no ordinary woman, not in the least. She was born Rebecca Goldstein to wealthy Jewish parents in a porch Northgate area of London, England. To many, she was known as Robbie. She too had various invisible friends that visited her on a daily bases, much to her alcoholic mother's annoyance, as Rebecca gradually distanced herself from dolls, skimpy cloths, make-up and the traditional role playing behaviors of little rich girls. Her mother always told friends: `She acts more like a man-child with her nasty little independent uppity self.' It really was not conceitedness, but rather mission focused attentiveness to what was most important at any point in time. Unwarranted jealousy was born and living a healthy life in the heart of hearts of her mother, who dominated her husband. Therefore, new plans had to be formulated to control Robbie after they found out that

105

she had an IQ of 156 at age ten. So shortly thereafter, her mother suggested that Robbie was crazy and needed therapy. She was mentally confused and doubting the spirit within, deeply conflicted by her parents professed love for her, while their behavior spoke volumes otherwise—her father, for his part, displayed incompetence as a politician, while sexually abusing her with the full knowledge of her mother, who ignored Robbie's black and blue-ridged backside from beatings and torture that was the father's doings. She never understood why he seemed to receive so much pleasure from such violent acts against his daughter, but was happy to see him happy while she cemented her scheme to do away with both of them. At thirteen, both parents decided to commit Robbie to a sanatorium, after she had confided in their Rabbi at the synagogue one Saturday. Unfortunately, the Rabbi had used the information to benefit himself. He used the 36 pictures of Robbie's battered black and blue body—obtained from the mother—to blackmail the father for a large sum of money: forcing him to resign from his political life as their constituents leading representative and promising back bencher in Parliament. Robbie remained drugged-up and isolated for three more years in an out-of-the-way Essex Asylum until discovery, by a different and more diligent younger psychiatrist assigned to her case. Dr. Goodwill was thorough in his assessments and examination of patients of the late Dr. Day. He quickly realized the flaws and lies in tests that were used by her manipulative parents, in concert with his bribed predecessor, to rid themselves of a brilliant child bent on reform. He could not change her past, but chose to provide some initial assistance. One night, just a week after her 16th birthday, Dr. Goodwill gave Robbie a one hundred pound note and released her into the dark and dreary streets of London. He had gone against the system to give her the drugless freedom she deserved. Immediately, Robbie changed her name for the first time. And just as quickly, she was swallowed up into a deadly prostitution ring by her greed driven Uncle, whom she contacted and thought trustworthy, one week after tasting freedom. For another seven years she had to wait on the spirit who sent an American to her rescue by marrying her right on the spot and carting her off to California. That 79 year old husband confided in her what her task was, dutifully informing her that this was his last mission before embracing the light of eternity.

And now Sister Love, as she passed the microphone to Sister Witch, looked up and joined the gaze of the gathering on the three hot air balloons above, surrounding the military blimp: This sign was one which signaled that it was time for the ultimate truth to come forth to all mankind.

"Thank you, thank you and thank you once again, all you for being here today. I'm Sister Witch. Yes, because ruthless, relentless, unscrupulous dictators have made your lives, our lives and life for each and every new child born, a bitch! I said a bitch not a beach, that's right! They have made life a bitch! It's not by happen chance that these greedy, life blood suckers have got thirty thousand seen and unseen satellites zeroed in on this spiritual meeting here today. It's no coincidence that there are three hot air balloons hovering over us right now. Let me tell you the truth. Two of them are carrying nerve gas and heat seeking missiles sufficient to eliminate all of us in a matter of seconds, if they are given the order by those destruction-driven dogs that would gladly kill each of us, if only we were only physical bodies and not vibrant earth conscious spirits. Can you dig it? They would and could—if allowed to—secretly, chemically dispose of our bodies within a matter of hours, minutes or seconds using anti-matter. That's right! But the third hot air balloon bearing the green earth symbol is the thriller. That right! It's the thriller! Look at it and you will see that it appear as if there is no one in it. That's true, except for the hundreds of thousands of angels of love that have rose up to protect us for the merciless! That's right! They have risen up to provide us with safe passage in our return to the promise land. They are going to scrub our earth clean. Moments ago, our pro Earth green hot air balloon has been ordered to move out of the air space above our meeting by the those two gutless military balloons. Those brutal military men, are blind to the powerful angels and spirit passengers on board that are poised in battle ready formation, on board our love this green air balloon. In fact, in our Blimp, which has circled by us twice, there are over 100,000 thousand souls who won't be bullied any further by the senseless enforcers of the system. So now, here is the question, what should we do about this impending threat to ourselves and our world? For it's all about love! Dig it! It's all about a loving defense of the righteousness in ourselves and our earth."

"Thank you very much Sister Witch, because this is it. We're gonna make an example of the change that each and every one of you will be duty bound to achieve within yourself and those that will be brought along to the promise land over the course of the next nine months, There'll be plenty of loving work to be done—restoration of the mind, body and spirit," said the Prophet. "That's right! The remedy is here and the time is now! I said, THE REMEDY IS HERE AND THE TIME IS NOW! Yes it's time to sow that lasting element of change in our hearts forever, as change agents of love. THIS IS IT! Here's what we're now guided to do. I want each and every one of you to take the hand of the person next to you, until we have a complete circular chain of connected people, spirits through which the energy of change will flow. Please be silent as you let your actions speak for themselves. That's right, I want every person who chooses to be responsible for playing a part in this history making moment—those committed to assuming responsibility to work towards reclaiming, redeeming and cleaning our plant—stand up and lock hands as we bind ourselves together forever through grace, in this historic spiritual revolution of peace. You all have three minutes to be sure that you are ready and a part of this transformation…and I don't want anyone to miss out on this experience. See, from that moment onward there will be no stopping us as we further the healing of this planet," bellowed the Prophet.

Gradually, people rose up and connected their hands. However, there seemed to be a proclamation of greater things to come in that hallowed tone that he used and the fact that, as he spoke two peculiar events seemed to happen simultaneously: the megaphone through which he spoke stayed afloat in front of his mouth without him holding it, as he connected his hands to the left with Sister Love and to the right with Sister Witch who at this point were levitating connected to him only by a hand in this chain of people.

But who was this mystical Sister Witch? When asked, she would quickly state that she was a helper for those that wondered in darkness so that they may see the light. She was born on board a 747 non-commercial liner given emergency clearance to land into the heart of Mongolia, where infant and mother were somehow stabilized inside a private hospital. Her parents were Russian diplomats to China returning to Moscow with top secrets about pending exploitive western affairs and operations in their care. So they were very surprised by the three-week early arrival of their daughter and extremely delighted after being given a clean bill of health. At three years of age she spoke six different languages fluently and happily predicted that an accident would excuse her from many great calamities that the world of China and Russia had to face, which shockingly included the demise of her parents. Their death declared an accident in a car where she was found unscratched but unconscious, happened 21 days later.

Little Julie was the only survivor that remained in a coma for 10 years. Every time they tried to illegally pull the plug on her, the person that tried, died. Four days after awakening, she quickly disappeared for another 14 years into Egypt and remerged in London, after five years of travel and mystical studies, only to live secluded within the bowels of West Minister Abby Cathedral for another seven years. That was where she was fed both physically and intellectually by a spirit guide called Hiram. That spirit promised and up to this moment had kept his promise to be with her always.

"Please keep your eyes closed and your hearts open. Relax! Enjoy the ride. We're now about to be transferred through glorious light, space and time along a peaceful pathway towards the promise land…in 5, 4, 3, 2, 1, BOOM!!!!!!"

THE MAKINGS OF A PSYCHIATRIST

Just past Columbus, Maryland, John "the perfect snoop" Albertson, with his puffy, slightly crooked left eye and infectious smile, swiftly dodged into Amtrak's train # 29 passenger sleeping car bound for Chicago. This was a very dangerous move for him—an economy class ticket-holding information magnet—because sleeping cars are off-limits to uninvited second class passengers. Bear in mind too, that despite having already billed his client for first class train and hotel accommodation, he chose to purchase traveling comforts of a lesser sort. If ill luck struck John and a crew-member caught him snooping, he would certainly be kicked off the train. However, despite the enormous pressures involved in deception, there was fame, fortune, and the talk show circuit to be had at the end of this special cross-country train ride. That is, so long as John turned in a verifiable and reliable project research report within the next thirty days. The goal was quite clear: Conclusively prove or disprove the therapeutic value of an Amtrak train ride.

Sweating heavily, John struggled to contain both his excitement and footing amid violent train gyrations, while advancing along the dimly lit corridor. Simultaneously, his mind reflected on the value of this research effort: It meant the difference between hundreds of millions of American dollars in funding increases or decreases for the entire Amtrak train system. Vividly, he remembered the strong admonition of his client: "We don't care how you get the statistics, man. Just get it! Get the hard cold facts. We need irrefutable evidence, one way or the other—fast! Cost is not a consideration, young man. For when Congress makes demands, we give it up," barked the freckle-faced aging Urban Mass Transportation director, only days before this nerve-wrecking train ride began.

Hours earlier within the Washington, D.C. Union Station train depot, John had easily connected with a pair of psychiatrists, a general contractor, a musician, two authors and their wives, whom he felt might well provide quality hard evidence. At that time, he was disguised as just another talkative, but bearable passenger—anxious and ready to get started on a journey. But now, where could those people he had targeted for his research be hiding? It is work time! Big money was on the line, he thought, as he gingerly inched down the hallway seeking his research subjects; yet his frantic mind screamed out at his racing heart, `Careful, you fool. You can't afford to arouse suspicion and blow this.´

Cautiously, John drifted past sleeper-room after sleeper-room straining to hear recognizable voices, armed with two hardly visible powerful microphones set to transmit back to his receiver and recorder at his seat. Suddenly, just up ahead, Dr. Elliot's booming German flavored voice cut across the small retiring voice of Dr. Jeffrey and immediately John's body froze. `Oh my god,´ his nervous system screamed at him, `You almost got caught with your pants down!´ Perspiration splattered freely from his forehead to his shoes. One quick glance revealed that their sleeper door was wide open, with only a half-curtain drawn across. Then with the microphones in hand, he timed the violent rocking of the train during one sharp almost-U-turn, and fell in onto the floor of their sleeper.

"Oh, my! Very sorry! Please pardon me," John said smiling as he foraged embarrassment.

His experienced abnormally long right arm—and using hands that were much faster than their eyes—allowed him to waste no motion. He had easily flipped one magnetized mike up under the reclining chair / bed and attached the other to the under-part of the table before breaking his fall and displaying an infectiously disarming smile.

"Listen", John continued throwing both empty hands up in the air as if helpless, "I lost my balance as this damn train lurched forward. Please forgive me." He comically shot them a wink from his jiggling, pinkish red and gray eye, along with his retarded looking signature smile, causing them to explode with laughter. Briskly, he added with laughter of his own, "My God, I lost my way and had a spill, before my first cocktail today!"

They seemed reasonably convinced that he was genuine and began to relax a little. Dr. Jeffrey was the first of the two to recover. She quickly apologized for their insensitivity in having laughed at his misfortune. But it was as Dr. Elliot assisted John to his feet that Dr. Jeffrey's memory went full circle.

She suddenly cried, "Hey! I know you. Wait a minute! Don't we know you from somewhere?"

"Why, yes! But, of course, right! You're the two Doctors from back at Union Station, in D.C. Yes! Now I remember—you guys are taking a break from the rat race for sanity's sake. Right?"

It was show time, as John's acting skills were being carefully studied by two curious pairs of bifocal-enriched microscope-like scientific eyes.

"Correct, you are indeed", said Dr. Elliot with a gracious smile, "Now then, is your sleeper near ours?" And without pausing to allow a response, "You know, we'd love to have you join us for dinner around 7:30 or so. Then you can tell us more about your research project. Does that work for you?" He glanced over at Dr. Jeffrey for her approval, which he got, with that ever so slight nod of her head.

"Well, as a matter of fact, I won't be using my sleeper much this trip", John replied, "That's because I will be up most of the time gathering research materials from passengers throughout the train." The part truth and part lie approach always seemed to work well, so he continued, "But I'd be happy to share a cocktail or two with you guys before we part company. How's that sound?

"Sure thing! We'll be here," returned Dr. Jeffrey.

Dr. Elliot spoke up, "You did say that you're going all the way to Albuquerque, too, aren't you?"

"Right you are. I'm trekking to Albuquerque, New Mexico, Salt Lake City, San Francisco, Utah, Yellow Stone National Park in Wyoming and Glacier International Peace Park in Montana. So I'm sure we'll be seeing each other real soon," John stated as he exited. Quickly, he made a bee-line to his coach seat, where he immediately began to check the quality of transmission from the planted mikes, tape recorder, and head-set. A mischievous smile played across John's face, as all devices seemed to be working well.

Behind much of both doctors' small talk recorded early that evening was one serious message: Dr. Jeffrey expected a breakthrough—some form of psychological awakening or rebirth—to occur during this train trip. Now that, to John, was the type of heavy stuff he could really sink his teeth into. Right here on Amtrak, therapeutic help was about to be administered and documented. This was irrefutable evidence for interested parties' to review, straight from two distinguished horses' mouths.

A little later, armed with laptop in hand, John slid into a lounge-car seat and researched both doctors, on Google. Dr. James Elliot was a brilliant psychiatrist and resident of Maryland State, licensed to practice in Maryland, Washington, D.C. and New York City. He specialized in treating psychologists and psychiatrists experiencing professional despair and burnout. Moreover, Dr. Sharon Jeffrey was nationally recognized for her genius in treating society's rich and famous. She was licensed to practice in California, Connecticut, Washington, D.C., New York, Chicago, Boston, and Virginia. They were certainly two big, big fish with a wealth of vital information.

James Leon Elliot had met Sharon Killroy Jeffrey at a Sweet Hearts ball in a New York State chartered chapter of a fraternity he was about to join. They were far from ever being doctors then and it was the University's Homecoming Ball night. After being stood up by an elegant happily married surgeon that Sharon wanted to bed, she slept with James Elliot on an 'only for tonight' basis. Fortunately for John, lonely people sometimes seem to bond as they wander aimlessly in and out of each other's lives.

They met and slept together again four years later, upon finding out that their careers intersected with the same Mormon adviser at a Salt Lake City University. The morning after that sexual experience, James felt certain he would never again be a competent lover and embrace the pleasures of this oversexed woman; he felt doomed to forever, only from a distance, love, worship, and obey her as need be. That same day, Sharon decided that they could only be dedicated friends and never try the sex thing again. Emphatically, they agreed to assist each other over and beyond the call of duty if ever there was a need. True friends for life, who would use whatever-it-took for the benefit of each other—if only he could control his strong secret urges for her loins stirring in his.

Goose pimples advanced across John's body, as he began an old breathing exercise from a past yoga class, in an attempt to stymie the tremendous excitement suddenly building within his chest. He focused on the rapidly disappearing foliage color patterns and rock and cloud formations, under the brilliant fading sunlight. Painstakingly, he attempted to contrast the spectacular scenery with that of the desert areas of his home state, Arizona, in hopes of redirecting his aroused sexual energies.

The train ride between Cumberland, Maryland, and Pittsburgh, Pennsylvania, displayed abundant spellbinding natural beauty. Sadly so, such magical splendor proved to be spiritually rejuvenating for only a hand full of observant passengers. But for most, as the sun receded under a raging high tide beneath bumpy tracks—influenced by a rapidly rising yellow full moon—all surreal possibilities and ominous things seemed to stir and become fully energized.

Upon entering the lounge car about 8:30 pm., John spotted both doctors seated at the far end. Other people were firmly wedged into the seats around them, so he just waved and they waved back. About ten minutes after John had sat down he saw Dr. Jeffrey suddenly appear disoriented, as first her head then her body slumped forward. To the discriminating eye, her skin had turned crimson red, her eyes bulged, and the corners of her drooling mouth twitched uncontrollably. Dr. Elliot calmly stated that Dr. Jeffrey was just quite tired and would be fine, as he quickly assisted *her* out of the car. John's heart began to race wildly as he sensed something big was happening. He rushed back to his coach seat and tuned on his listening devices. Sweating profusely, he waited for what felt like forever until the doctors reached their sleeper.

"Oh my God!"

"Yes, Jeffrey"

"Elliot! Damn! Man, I think it's happening. I feel like I'm beginning to lose myself in it—something of a breakthrough. Lots of old painful images are flashing by beyond my control from deep within me—it's quite a mess…I, I, think we're going to have to sort through it all somehow," said Dr. Jeffrey while seating herself on the bed and looking around cautiously before continuing, "It is true. So true…my goodness, we do naturally and normally go from mental breakdown through breakthrough to recovery. Right, Doctor?" Her statements seemed consistent with the new rich red color on her glistening face washed in tears and her distant looks that only James understood.

From the tangled knots of tension pains in the pit of his stomach, John knew that this was it. Something monumental was happening. In fact, about thirty minutes ago, John had clearly seen when Dr. Elliot had slipped two pink and gray pills into Dr. Jeffrey's drink. Psychiatrists are used to using drugs to treat diagnosed patients, aren't they? But should drugs be used to aid in determining the degree of one's mental illness? Though drug induced, had all information hurdles been cleared and no way of turning back left open for either doctor?

"That's great," Dr. Elliot responded, "Now, let's make you as comfortable as possible, darling. There! There! You're just fine! Now, if you will please start wherever you want. And remember, during this regression, I'm with you every step of the way. It's an honor and my duty to show you true respect, warm love, and appreciation. Please begin wherever you like."

"James! Oh James, it's such a great big mess, oh God—I see it all!" Her voice wobbled terribly as hot tears tumbled down her cheeks.

"I guess it began when I was born: I was faced with the challenge of being quite bright, financially well-off, but physically different. Most of the time, I was a tomboy right from the start. Now, I feel like an old, despicable, washed up hermaphrodite—plain and simple. Back then, I was alive yet a different child, confused in terms of which bathroom to use, colors to wear and searching to find out who I was supposed to be. Ah, Christ, ah…which gender's behavior was I to use at church gatherings, around older affluent members of our prestigious family and community. I wanted to fit in permanently—somewhere. My curse, James, was not the plague or an infectious disease, just the burdensome task of being both boy and girl at once. It was pure hell! My god, you just don't understand…"More tears rushed down over ever-expanding dark swollen bags under her eyes. Desperately, amid sobs she fought for clarity and control, sufficient to continuing.

"I'd hide away many times for long periods locked in worlds created by great authors displayed within their books, searching for normality. By age ten, I was an honor student and a disruptive class clown. Desperately, I clung to the harsh pain of feeling like a freak of nature…and still the teacher's pet!" Dr. Jeffrey paused trembling and crying in the moment, as she gladly used the tissues offered by Dr. Elliot.

"Life was a mess in our upper-class, Chicago, East Side home. It was one big stinking mess! The elders in our large family knew of my affliction, but never treated me differently until puberty. The secret was that two or three hermaphrodites were born into our family every other generation. It's like hypertension in black families: the disease that generally skips family members of one generation and caught the next. But no one told me anything. One big mess…"she sobbed and sobbed but bravely continued, "I see it all now as a great sadness—one big mess around dishonest people.

118

As my breasts began to come in most family members looked at me oddly, and the truly gracious ones only snickered behind my back. I was the butt-end of family jokes to all except for my older brother, Johnny. But he was a bastard too, in so many ways. He stood up for me even at the cost of losing all of his biweekly allowance money—cursing and threatening lives like a sea-hardened sailor. Ah, I guess you could say in a way, Uncle Matt did in some ways try to be a buffer, too, up to a point. Jesus Christ! He was a weird son-of-a-bitch!" Fighting hard to contain herself, she continued, "See, it seemed like those two men didn't believe that having both sex organs was a sin, nor was it a violation of anyone's constitutional rights." Dr. Jeffrey paused, her eyes closed, trembling while reliving past trauma for another five or six watery minutes.

Dr. Elliot tried to urge her on, "So, how does your dual gender difference make you feel? Tell me, more. Yeah. Ah, and just a little bit more please, about Johnny and Uncle Matt. And do feel free to express how you feel they might have influenced the way you have felt all of your life, Sharon—bringing you to this point"

"Yes, yes. James, in just a few words, this is awful and they were really horrible to me. I have felt and do still feel quite inadequate, unloved, bisexual, strange, abused, scared, rebellious, lonely, superior or inferior and now completely mentally lost." She readjusted her position on the bed and frantically reached out feeling for her cigarette case.

"No, no. Please," said Dr. Elliot as he took her hand in his and squeezed it gently, "Not just yet, darling. Shall we wait a bit for the break-through to take its course? That is, before we take a smoke break? Shall we? Please, darling? That would be quite splendid, I'd say."

"Oh, ok, James, I know you would know best about these things. Well, it was on the Saturday of one Memorial Day

119

weekend when I lost my virginity to Uncle Matt, the family's big-time jeweler. It happened in a wooded area not too far from where our family's annual picnic took place near Lake Michigan. I had just turned fourteen. The truth is that I'm still damn mad about that mess with Uncle Matt. That dirty *fucker*! He always showed a great interest in me, especially when I was studying those anatomy and physiology books from my father. In fact, my family had used Uncle Matt to act as a surrogate father to me, after Dad's death, when I was only seven. My father was a nationally respected surgeon who, at age forty, fell victim to a killer aneurysm." Her tears were flowing real fast now as she hugged herself releasing low groans intermittently.

Silently, Dr. Elliot reassuringly stroked her hand as he passed her new clumps of tissue—desperately resisting the burning urge to hold her close, protectively and kiss her.

"It, it was a case of plain rape, dear God..."Dr. Jeffrey continued, I never consented to letting Uncle Matt touch me that way. Up till then, I really liked him. He was my favorite uncle. I really trusted him. But he was on the prowl and I was an easy target—a temptation he just couldn't pass up. Hell! My family had left the rat to guard and protect the cheese. Fucking fools!"

Dr. Elliot suddenly snatched his hand away, stood up, and said, "Darling, now, I want you to relax and hold still for just one moment. I have to run get some more boxes of tissue. Just lay quietly. I'll be back in a flash." Dr. Elliott came back so quickly she didn't have enough time to find her cigarette case and light a cigarette.

"Please go on," he commanded her as he handed her more tissue.

"It was a blustery overcast day. I was peacefully meandering through the shrubbery and tall grasses just off from Lake Michigan; about a mile or two away from where everyone was picnicking. I wanted to be alone to sort out why Uncle Matt had been recently pinching, pulling, squeezing, and patting on my body parts when no one was looking. I had to decide whether to tell Mother or not. Johnny told me later that Uncle Matt noticed I was missing and promptly volunteered to find and bring me back to the picnic. I was picking some wild flowers when he rushed up panting, grabbed me and started mouth-kissing and feeling me up. His rough lips and tongue smothered the scream trapped deep within my throat. I was horrified. I resisted but he was stronger. Jesus Christ!" She moaned, as more tears bathed her face, but she continued courageously.

"Uncle Matt roared, 'Girl, you better drop your pants, or I'll drop it for you. Right now!' With an unnatural glare protruding from his eyes."

"No! No! Not you! You're my uncle, I yelled yanking my arm away. Uncle Matt pulled out his little four-inch-blade pocketknife, shoving it against my carotid artery and bellowed: 'You're going to do it. And you're going to do it, now —or I'll kill you! If you scream no one will hear you. And you've got better sense than that, I know. Now, lay down! And lay still. You know I've been in love with you forever.' I saw red. But I was pinned-down, trembling and too scared to move. I did as I was told. O my…God."

"Well, his hand went down there. And when Uncle Matt felt that I was hard as he was yet juicy in the other part, his eye grew wide with shock. He seemed paralyzed with fear. I'll never forget that moment. His sweaty face lost all color as his tongue and mouth fought to properly channel air trapped deep within. Then he shouted, 'My God! What is this damnation? I never believed the family's gossip about you. Your Aunt May was like this. And I did her too. I'm going to fix it for you now, baby. Hell, I'm going to bust your sweet young cherry.' You should have seen that big

121

smile on his stupid looking face." More tears and tissues were quickly exchanged between the doctors.

"That's when he hurt my insides real bad...'Jesus! Stop! Stop! Stop Gad-damn-met! That hurts! Please stop hurting me, Uncle. Please. I begged as he continued to hurt me so bad. But he was enjoying himself too much to release me. That no good son-of-a-bitch!" Then a river of tears shot down Dr. Sharon Jeffrey's face, as she wept bitterly for what seemed like an eternity reliving the experience.

"It was then that I realized that I would not be able to walk straight in front of everyone at the picnic that day—all because of that big, fat, sloppy, no-good son of a bitch! Bastard!"

Dr. Jeffrey stopped and laid still for about 8 or 9 minutes, pampering and slowly gained control of herself, before she resumed. And in his economy class seat, John beamed with joy over the treasures he had found.

"'This is our secret for life, honey buns! Remember me as your special one! I made you a woman today,' Uncle Matt muttered as he ejaculated in me. 'Take this as a token of my love for you, you pretty blue eyed devil,' he yelled cheapening me more by dropping a two karat almost flawless diamond ring into my palm after I had wiped myself up as best I could. He continued,' Well, it's no use in getting mad and telling anyone. This is our little secret. Remember that! Keep your mouth shut and I'll give you anything you want.' I smiled bitterly, inwardly determined to make him pay for the pain in my groin. I quickly pocketed the ring and tried to act normal as we approached the picnic area."

"Suddenly, I felt dirty and riddled with guilt while reflecting back on how I used to sit on Uncle Matt's lap and wondered if my innocent play with him might have been the cause of what happened. I felt scared and was sure that everyone was looking me over closely and knew what had just transpired between us. O

God, I really wanted to die. I quickly whispered to my mother that I was having very bad cramps and needed to go home. Mother seemed quite surprised, because she knew I had just finished my menstrual at the beginning of the week. Decisively, Johnny stated that he would gladly walk those twelve blocks back home with me. But no, Uncle Matt offered to drive me home, and that's when I clung on to Johnny. Mother decided that Johnny should spend the day at home with me and that Uncle Matt would only drive us there." She paused briefly as Dr. Elliot handed her more tissue.

"Then my life began to speed up. Johnny sensed something had happened to me that day, but accepted my bad cramps theory. In fact, after I had soaked and showered for almost three hours, Johnny and I began what became our ritual. We spent that entire afternoon and at least three or four hours after school daily, laying-together, cuddling and caressing each other gently. Our behavior had psychologically crossed the line into a too-close-for-comfort male-female intimacy. I was healing my insides while vigorously interrogating Johnny on how much he knew about the art and science of making love. He was plum green. Two weeks of this tabooed intimacy with Johnny and then I took his virginity. It was so amazing to see the once nervous boy, my brother, transformed from babbling idiot into a man."

She blew her nose loudly, "I was contentedly enjoying Johnny as my new toy, when Uncle Matt came barging back into my life one rainy afternoon. He picked me up right after school that day. Immediately, he dropped a two carat ruby ring into my hand and an envelope with two thousand dollars in it. Tearfully, he apologized for what had happened a month before. We ended up at first in the back seat of his Jaguar and later at a motel. Gone were those feelings of guilt and the anger of having been violated. Intercourse was not so bad this time, especially, after his apology, the second ring, and the hefty pocket change," she stated more calmly.

"Well, Johnny was in a big rage when I got home that night. He had searched my room and found the diamond ring and stood there accusing me of being with another lover. First, I made him give me back my diamond ring. I let him know that he did not own me, nor was he my husband or father. I was not his property and had done him—a big dumb sixteen-year-old man without a girlfriend—a favor by giving him some. And that he would not get any more for a very long time because of his outlandish fits of jealousy. I also reminded him that if mother was informed about what he was making me do sexually, he would be dead meat. Johnny calmed down quickly, and tried to sweet-talk me back into bed for the next two months, but it didn't work. I was busy filling my coffers with jewelry and big money, planning to be something special when this was over. Because it all just had to end real soon."

"Then I missed my period. I was angry and confused. And quickly decided, if shit was going to hit the fan, then I was going to make sure that everyone got dirty and went down with me, if and when I crashed. So I gave one grateful Johnny some great loving, just before I faced Uncle Matt with the dreadful news. But, that same evening, I also found out why my uncle never remarried after his wife had died ten years ago. My uncle Matt, that's right, he got down on all fours and asked for my forgiveness, as he took my thing like his and nursed it for a while. He begged me to put it in him. So I took charge, turned him around and did him like he wanted it. He seemed to have more fun with me doing him than the other way around. Pure girlishness flowed out of his every pore as he pranced and bucked joyfully. Yes, the shocking truth was quite unnerving. My entire family was a pack of fucking weirdoes." Dr. Jeffrey sat up and quickly blew her nose before gently relaxing back on the bed.

"Over dinner that evening, Uncle Matt tearfully begged me not to give birth to our child. He knew the truth would mean his sudden death by some outraged family members. Somberly, he promised to make the necessary arrangements for my abortion. I was shaking with fear when I got home and frantically climbed into Johnny's strong arms that night. While in need of reassurance and guidance, two unpleasant things happened: Uncle Matt's name escaped my lips as Johnny and I were having sex. And secondly, I blamed Johnny for making me pregnant. Johnny carefully beat me up that night: first in my stomach, on my back, and finally my upper thighs where no one would easily notice, if I wore a short dress. He swore to find out about this Uncle Matt intimate business with me and kill him, if necessary. It was a very bad scene but I couldn't talk to no one, so I cried myself to sleep under three layers of thick blankets, with help from a couple of Darvon pills."

Dr. Jeffrey stopped talking as she was signaled to Dr. Elliot that she thought she had heard someone outside, so he quickly looked outside the room door and locked it again. He motioned and whispered for her to continue while offering her his best reassuring smile. A subdued Dr. Jeffrey, only laid there and cried softly for a while, gathering her wits about her.

"Johnny! Poor, Johnny. He didn't sleep home that night. And Moms stayed up all night worrying, unsure of what was going on. Then bright and early the next morning, Uncle Matt came by and gave me the address to go to for the abortion. On the receipt he gave me were the words *Paid in Full*, stamped in bold red letters. And as uncle Matt was leaving down the stairs, Johnny came up and demanded that they take a drive together, NOW! That was the last time I ever saw either man alive." For the next seven minutes,

125

Dr. Jeffrey wept and Dr. Elliot just let her; for as she laid there trembling and releasing, he felt his strong physical need for her building.

"Uncle Matt and Johnny were found naked and dead in Uncle Matt's home the next morning. They were found during those painful moments following my abortion: we learned that they had passed away about eight hours earlier, so when I was bleeding my life away like crazy last evening, the two greatest loves of my life were dying. Oh God...I was totally devastated. I still am, very, very angry over this mess, in fact...We understood that an inebriated Uncle Matt had died of obvious strangulation by Johnny while in the throes of some extremely gratifying tabooed sexual act. The Coroner's report stated that Uncle Matt had been subjected to quite a beating and sodomy prior to submitting to a seemingly enjoyable death. And poor drunken Johnny had committed suicide rather than face the charges that were sure to follow." Dr. Jeffrey paused and drank the glass of water extended to her by Dr. Elliot. Then she vigorously wiped her bloated red eyes while attempting to stem the flow of tears.

"Everyone save for my mother thought the pain of losing my only brother was the sole reason for my severe depression and extended bedridden state. But my God, my God, why me? I had lost three: a baby, a brother and an uncle in less than twenty-four hours. I was high as a kite from an old sock full of various tranquilizers and drugs, which I had collected since my first very painful menstrual cycle, a few years ago. The shame and overpowering guilt was too much for me to handle with a straight face. In later years, it became clear that all the members of my family, if not openly, lived a double life: straight in one performance and gay as hell in the other. All I wanted to be was normal. And finally, I am having a mental breakdown over someone else's similar problem...It's truly insane, isn't it?"

"No! No, no. In fact," began Dr. Elliot, "It's quite possibly a very near natural human response that's happening here. Now tell me, who provided that similar stimuli?"

"Look. Dr. Elliot, I've got to stop and have a cigarette, a drink, and some time to recharge my batteries. There is more, I promise. Believe me. I now know that it was a feeling of responsibility for three deaths at once which compelled me to become a psychiatrist." Dr. Jeffrey quickly sat-up and slipped down off the bed, retrieved and lit a cigarette.

"That's fine, darling. I'd say we have some breakfast and resume when we're on the next train to Albuquerque. How about that?"

"That's great! And don't you dare keep me away from my cigarettes for damn-near eight hours again, ok!" Dr. Jeffrey dried her face some more and half smiled as she pushed her hair back, "And thank you ever so much, James, I know you really care," she added.

"Agreed," Dr. Elliot replied and continued, "You were absolutely splendid. And, you've made great progress—great strides indeed. I do believe I just heard the steward in passing say Hammond, Indiana is our next stop. Super! Hey, we're real close to Chicago now, you know." Dr. Jeffrey only nodded and inhaled deeply. "Oh, and while we're in Chicago, please think on what recent incident may have sparked this voyage back to the painful setting of your pubescent years, will you?"

***

After almost eighteen hours into this research effort, Amtrak's train, The Capitol Limited, squealed to a halt in the Windy City. People impatiently bumped, pushed and squeezed pass each other, in their hurried attempts to disembark. At 41 bone-chilling degrees, the weather seemed to be playing a brutal game; first it was raining in blinding torrential sheets around 10:00 a.m., assiduously retarding arriving passengers advance into downtown Chicago. The icy rain they could manage, but that fierce skin-shredding wind, seemingly well below freezing, was a bit much.

Shortly after 11:00 a.m., the sun appeared from behind gloomy dark-gray clouds as the sleet began to subside and a noticeable calm crept over the restless crowd at the front door of The Chicago Art Institute. But by 11:45 a.m., the temperature had suddenly dipped to 28 degrees, as gusty winds approaching gale force strength pounded thick snow-flakes into the eyes, noses, and throats of all those outside.

Four long hours remained before two doctors and John—friends at least for the duration of this trip—would electronically reunite on train # 3 (the same train with a different number) heading south to Albuquerque. John contemplated whether viewing wonderful old paintings would distract him enough for his mind to rest. Because he was dying to know more and have the doctor's complete story in hand, time just seemed to stand still. The idea of finishing up one phase of his strictly confidential research on using train-rides as therapy—by documenting the second part of a psychiatrist's life—delighted him to no end. Thank God, John thought, the doctors would never know of his recorded dark deeds or so he hoped. Cold, unsettling shivers ran down his spine.

Filled with euphoria, John paused outside the Chicago Art Institute to decide on which major art exhibit he would see. There was a famous 16th century French portrait painter, a rural 19th century Black-foot Indian exhibit or the works of the fine American landscape realist, Frederick Church. Immediately, John entered the line that extended almost to the street to view Mr. Church's exhibit. Just then, three excited old men, two Oriental and one Caucasian, rushed up and begged John to shoot their pictures with a disposable camera. John honored their request, and they all but fell over each other thanking him for documenting their first reunion after 55 years.

***

The previous evening, at the beginning of his train ride from Washington, D.C. to Chicago, John had found himself saddled with some frightfully peculiar and somewhat insufferable individuals. Upon boarding the train he found the seat issued to him by the conductor located between three intimidating looking black individuals. The two black men seated together viewed John with hostile glares, while the black woman and her bags took up her seat and the adjacent aisle seat, which rightfully belonged to John. As John stood there all eyes met and he said, "Excuse me," three times, hoping the black woman would get the message. She just sat there clicking some chewing gum, seemingly consumed with madness, as she rolled her eyes at him menacingly.

The closest man to John bellowed, "What's up, chief?"

At that point, John fought to contain his anger. "If she's your woman, you need to inform her that she'd better move into her seat and move her butt and bags out of my aisle seat immediately," John stated boldly drawing up his entire six feet four inch frame in an intimidating manner over them and reducing the quality of his language befitting to his audience. She moved quickly, while cursing under her breath, supported by her two grumbling male companions.

Fifteen minutes later as John's three black seat-mates started down the aisle scowling, the thickset man who had muttered something to John earlier said, "Chief, I'm leaving my bags here, look out for them, for us, ok?"

John said, "It's Mr. Albertson, not Chief. And your name is?" The man walked away bitterly mumbling something about you white folks under his breath.

The short skinny man turned and said, "We're just going to the snack bar, ok!" John chose to ignore the little guy. This gave him time to extract his work equipment (microphones, head set, and tape recorder) and check once again the sound level and recording tape space available for any information transmitted.

Fifteen minutes later when they returned John said, "Please check your bags, your cheap looking bags, that is, and see if everything is as you left it, sirs."

"Thanks, Chief. I appreciate it," said the burly man.

John stated firmly, "its Mr. Albertson to you. And as a matter of fact, it's clearly insane for you to believe that someone, especially me, would steal your baggage," pausing briefly, "I don't play that mess, Buster!" And loudly with sarcasm, John unloaded just before he started to walk away, "Oh, it's a full moon tonight and I should expect this from a resident loony!" It was only after that cutting mental exchange that John was able to peacefully wander off in search of his possible research subjects and begin his work in earnest.

***

Just minutes before arriving at their destination, Hammond, Indiana, John's previously ill-mannered seatmates suddenly displayed an attitudinal and behavioral metamorphosis of sorts.

The little stocky man leaned over and said, "Hey sir, sir, can I ask you a question?"

Rather cautiously John took his head set off his ears and said, "Yes."

"Tell me, where did you buy your camping gear? It looks great and, I hear that JanSport is a good name brand. Is it as good as they say it is, man?" he inquired.

John agreed with the man, and added "In fact, my backpack's guaranteed for life by JanSport." Additionally, John informed him of where he had purchased it.

And before they knew what had happened, they had started talking about the economy, politics and social plight of disunited black Americans, hillbilly poor white folk, harmful white solidarity groups, poor housing affecting all races in supposedly the greatest and most wasteful nation in the world. Of course, everyone in that car began pitching in with their comments, now that they felt at ease in a discussion with a seemingly, somewhat educated individual. In that instance, John discovered that although Thomas, the thickset black fellow, had been born in Miami, his father was a Bahamian. Thomas revealed that he had lived in Nassau, Bahamas, for a few years while growing up. John immediately understood why this group of somewhat small-minded individuals had responded with such intense hatred, insecurity and fear towards him. The lady vehemently declared that to her, anyone from a big city was suspect, especially those from Washington, D.C.—death-city, U.S.A. 1991-1995. Ironically, John too hailed from Abaco in The Bahamas—although he now was a dual citizen of both countries.

With Chicago well behind us and Albuquerque as our destination on board train # 3, The South West Chief, fatigue's deep sleep quickly descended upon many passengers. And although two hours of proper rest was all John had gotten, it would have to suffice. Three hours out of Chicago, the rails became excessively bumpy and frightening to a number of children, whose shrill voices reaffirmed their disapproval to most adults. John's silent listening device notified him that there was no activity between the two doctors; at least not in the room where he had placed the microphones. Or could they have found his microphones by accident and destroyed them?

The reputed party scene of the lounge car was in full swing around nine o'clock that evening as riding conditions had improved considerably. Some people played cards, backgammon, monopoly or tick-tack-toe. Others drank, smoked, snacked, read, conversed or watched a movie. The heighten jubilation in this packed car demonstrated that the inescapable blue moon had not yet relinquished it's powerful grip on all aboard.

John took the only available seat at a table facing a black woman named Cora, about age 40, whose alcohol-drenched brain had reduced her to nothing more than one big trick. Cora sat in the middle of three large and loud shady-looking hillbilly-acting white men. They seemed to be guardedly drunk and cautiously distrustful of any intruder. In her unsavory attempts to enjoy achieving complete inebriation, Cora became very loud, common and increasingly unattractive. Yet, she constantly bragged about her two boys who were traveling with her, as if they were her only love interest.

John casually asked," Well, why aren't your boys here in this car with you instead of present company?"

"Yeah! See, 'cause they understand, their Ma needs time to have some fun and make some money. Oh, I gave each of 'em two shots of Gin and that will keep them sleep until morning."

John's mouth fell wide open in shocked disbelief of such blatant child abuse.

"Close your mouth, honey-pie, you're goin' catch flies in it if you don't," said Cora.

Immediately, one of those classless guys at the table stood up and announced that he was going to get more drinks. Cora told him what she wanted and John declined.

"Honey," she said to John after three more free drinks from these sleaze-balls, "I'll be ready! Hell! I'm hot, and I aim to have me some fun, and collect me some money for my boys…Now how you want it? I'm satisfaction guaranteed, my brother!"

Thinking it appropriate to offer advice, John said to Cora, "I believe you're kidding. And, I really think it's time for you to go get some sleep, young lady."

"Oh, no, not till I throw some of this good pussy on you, or whatever you want. Don't be shame! You can be my brother, too!"

As John visually reviewed this group, the tobacco-chewing fat thug-like scared face man with a mouth full of rotten teeth said, "She's serious, man! She's a darn good hooker. I mean a real-good hooker, my man! Hell, she got us all off in less than ten minutes. By Golly, she did me and Jack together, then did Joe by himself. Just get her in one of them twin bathrooms down stairs and you'll get everything you need."

Cora quickly spoke up, "Alright play brother, your time to buy me two drinks, ok? Then we go do the wild thing, right?"

"No thank you, Madame," John said as he stood up.

Cora yelled, "Come on, white boy, let me give you some relief. Don't tell me you ain't got no money, cause, you wouldn't be traveling without no fun money!"

"God bless you and your little boys, lady," said John as he threw a 10 dollar bill towards her and left abruptly. His mind was bent on the soon to come main attraction between the two psychiatrists. It just had to happen tonight, he thought.

133

John was not quite ready for bed and took one of two now vacant seats further along in the lounge car. Almost immediately, he found that taking this seat was also a mistake. The welcoming Spanish man sitting opposite to him proved to be an abusive drunk who snapped at his son every few minutes and diabolically cursed any and everyone who looked at him with disdain. Carlos was obviously very bitter about his life. He quickly regurgitated his woes to John in hopes of receiving another drink. But only seconds after John was seated, he received a stern warning from both the conductor and bartender. Therefore, he promptly refused to purchase any liquor for Carlos. Unfortunately for Carlos, he had been barred from having or being allowed to purchase more liquor that night, which agitated him to no end.

Nonetheless, Carlos enthusiastically re-told his story to all within earshot, while verbally mistreating his son.

"My damned wife ran off with my best friend—a big white two faced fucker that worked with me, called Joe. Well, first off, she started being with him, when I was at work. That's right, that white motherfucker started taking days off and spending money on her, while I was hard at work. And after work, I'd came home to hell and pure pain from that woman, who had laid on her ass all day. Oh yeah! She found every which way possible to show me how much she hated me and why I should be a man and leave my son and just go! `Just go! She'd say, just go!´ Then like the scum that she is, she left my son with me six months ago and ran off to Mississippi with that bastard. Well, six weeks ago she called me and begged my forgiveness, for the sake of our son. She told me to come and bring our son down to Mississippi, where I could easily get a good construction job. Yeah! She said it. She said, she was through with being a bad girl...We could be a family again. And that we shouldn't just throw six years away like that. Well! I

134

packed up everything I had in this world and moved me and my son to Mississippi. That's when she dumped me again. In just three days. Damn! So I worked four weeks to get enough money to take this train back to Los Angeles. And I've been drinking ever since I got our tickets."

Carlos finally became so obnoxious that two attendants and the conductor both gave him a final warnings to go sleep and stop the cussing which showed disrespect for everyone else. This all happened within a forty-five minute period. Finally, the train stopped in a dark field outside Kansas City where they grabbed Carlos and unceremoniously put him off the train. They laid rough hands on Carlos across his chest and backside with a cat-o-nine tail and was about to leave him out there when the tearful pleas of his seven-year old son convinced them to rescind their vengeful deed. So they swiftly bound and gagged Carlos and placed him in a room by himself, where he was forced to enjoy an alcohol-free sleep.

John was shutting the lounge car's door—headed for his economy car seat—when he looked back and noticed the two doctors. They only looked into the lounge car and quickly retreated into the direction of the sleeper cars. A wave of shame swept over him. John felt guilty about the lethal personal information he had gathered from them and didn't want to face them over drinks. Sensing that they had not noticed him, he quickened his steps to his seat. Silently trembling with anticipation, he waited for further input, while reminding himself that he was only doing his job.

Barely ten minutes had passed before the thick, nerve-wrecking silence was broken by calming familiar voices in his headset.

"Dr. Elliot, I do believe I am up to the task of unburdening myself further with the answers you wanted earlier," said Dr. Sharon Jeffrey.

135

"Very well. But first let's have ourselves a good drink of water, shall we?" replied Dr. Elliot, as he quickly served up spring water. "Now, let's begin again. Only this time I want you to recall the stimuli within the last week or so, which sent your mind back to the trauma of your early adult life. Ok?"

"Yes, doctor," Dr. Jeffrey began, "Well, it was one of the original members of The Jackson Four + 1's great-granddaughter-in – law's story that broke the camel's back for me." Gratefully, she took another big swig of water from the glass he had just refilled.

"Stephanie Cartwright-Jackson was on time for her second session with me. She was an insecure hermaphrodite who had not been lynched or crammed into one role or another. But it was the abuse of her human dignity by her great-grandfather-in-law at age ten that got to me. He showed no remorse even when she took him to court. This too had troubled her for the past sixteen years. Stephanie felt that her entire adult life had been a mass of relationship disasters. All the family knew what he had done to Stephanie, but refused to stand up for her against great-granddad's big money." She started to reach for her cigarette case but just as quickly Dr. Elliot stopped her.

"Well then, when Stephanie was only half through her story, I found myself in tears. I shouted, `Fuck it! Fuck the dumb Shit´ In a rage, I ran to my vault and opened it violently. I pulled out my colt forty-five semi-automatic and yelled, `We're not going to take this abuse no more! Let's go! Let's get it on! I'll stand up for you and kill the nasty, stinking, son-of-a-bitch! No! You don't have to take this shit sitting down, girlfriend. Hell! I want his ass. I want to drink his frigging blood! NOW! Stephanie screamed, frozen solid and drenched with tears, as I was waving the gun around wildly. That's when Charlotte—my Jamaican secretary—rushed in pleading and begging, with eyes ballooned big as a saucer."

"'Dr. Jeffrey! Oh no! No. God-in-heaven, help us…Doctor, put that damned gun down, now! Now! I said put it down, now! Come on. Just you sit down—both of you—this minute! There is nothing in this world more important than your mental health,' said Charlotte as she slapped me silly and calmly took the gun from me. It was only then that I realized that I needed help fast." Dr. Jeffrey's hands were shaking as she pressed the glass of water to her lips and emptied it—as snot and tears blended together across twittering ruby-red cheeks.

"Rest, now. You must rest yourself, darling. I am quite proud of you, Dr. Jeffrey," said Dr. Elliot, slipping back into the present from the edge of the past, silently longing for her love, but somehow managing to restrain himself, "But since it is very late, I'll give you my short, summary comments. Then you can freshen up in the toilet. And of course, I will be treating you while we're in Albuquerque. So here goes. You don't seem to have found peace with yourself concerning the three deaths in your past. Nonetheless, society is much better off because of those early pains that propelled you into becoming a worthwhile psychiatrist. Now, I do believe that you were subjected to great abuses in your early childhood similar to those of Stephanie. And you somehow unconsciously identified with her resentment of the physical and mental abuses—similar to your own—which she might have been a victim of. Therefore, I sincerely want to encourage you to accept responsibility for your part in each moment of pleasure and abuse in your life. You are not a victim, but a competent decision-maker, one who can now decide how best to take charge of every aspect of your future. Do it! You can't change your past, but you can forgive yourself for your part in your past and can now continue to make a difference in your future. Do you understand me?"

"Yes, yes. Thank you, James. You, you're really a good doctor, you know. And you're absolutely right. I thank you for being there

137

for me and taking me on such short notice. But, now, it's smoke time. And like most non-smokers, you don't understand my needs in that way, I'm sure," said Dr. Jeffrey.

"True enough and it's past your bed time, darling. I'll give you a sedative that should allow you to sleep until we reach Albuquerque, as soon as you're finished with the toilet and your smoke." replied Dr. Elliot.

***

Sunday morning arrived quickly under rich blue New Mexico skies. John had a story that would knock the socks off the bigwigs at Amtrak. He first had to make a presentable copy of this tape— all names removed. Additionally, he needed three other pieces of hard evidence.

Shortly after 11:00 a.m., John started his day by consuming a cup of tea and two very tasty tomato sandwiches. Then just after 3 o' clock he ate two more tomato sandwiches, only this time, in the lounge car. He was all but half way through eating the second sandwich, when Ms. Broomsted, the female attendant, pulled-up on him abruptly and inquired, "So, tell me, did you buy either of those sandwiches at the Lounge Café, sir?"

"Neither," John replied. He was being truthful for once. The expensive lounge car Café did not sell tomato sandwiches nor blue cheese on a bun.

The female attendant continued, "Well, did you at least buy that soda or coffee from us, sir?"

"Madame, maybe I did and maybe I didn't. Now be gone with yourself," John replied dismissively.

"Well, let me make this perfectly clear to you, sir. Only passengers who buy food at our Café can sit and eat at tables in this lounge car," she stated vehemently.

138

Obviously, it was a stupid policy and a stupid decision to approach John with such madness. He angrily informed her that there was next to no choice of places to purchase food from or places where he could sit and eat on this train, out in the middle of nowhere. Also, if Amtrak was willing to allow unrestricted clouds of smokers' stench to engulf both the non-smoker's and smoker's areas in the lounge car, then, as a paid ticket holder he was entitled to sit and eat his provisions in the lounge car.

Losing ground rapidly as more passengers witnessing the incident began to congregate, the attendant countered, "The reason we use that rule, sir, is because when you eat in the lounge car, and we see you eating there, if something happened to you, like food poisoning, we can quickly verify your claim of having eaten food from the Café." John clearly pointed out that her statements were both ludicrous, disrespectful and an attempt to grandstand while enforcing a ridiculous policy, if such did exist.

The mountains outside Taos silently reduced themselves slightly around Apache Crossing, and Red Earth Valley gradually evened out into glorious flat land between Lamy and Albuquerque. It was 4:55 p.m. when they arrived on time in Albuquerque.

Nevertheless, nothing was easy for them. In fact, they experienced a bit of a scare about one hour before their arrival. While ascending the Rodaira mountains, both of the supposedly new engines got too hot to climb further up that very steep incline. The train started to roll backwards and came to an unexplained abrupt halt in the middle of nowhere. On display was an assortment of dangerous snakes just outside the windows, lazily stretched out, sunning themselves along rocky ledges. In contrast, a few miles away, splashed across a plush green valley floor, were hundreds of Black-Angus cattle grazing contentedly. Some minutes later, the conductor's calming voice attempted to ease passengers' anxiety by informing them that Amtrak's new engines needed to cool down for twenty minutes or so, before attempting to finish climbing this mountain ridge. Some passengers kept their fingers crossed while others held their breath, and finally they resumed their trek across this mountainous peak, reaching an elevation of 7,900 feet.

During the last hour and a half before arriving in Albuquerque, John met an underwriter from Maine who urged him to visit Maine in August. There is one spectacular lobster eating festival experience to be had. This gentleman, wholeheartedly recommended the therapeutic value in riding on Amtrak. Mark felt that the way to manage his fear of flying while still enjoying solace from the stress of everyday city-life was by riding Amtrak. John had easily learned a lot from him about Maine's hidden, undisturbed and beautiful noteworthy natural scenery. And once again, all of what Mark had shared, John had ruthlessly used his pocket-recorder to capture without consent. With this information, John was determined to investigate, experience and stockpile photographs and sketches of Bar Harbor and the Schoodic Peninsula Acadia National Park in the state of Maine.

Moments later, John met James Wilson—an artist from Detroit, Michigan—who shared numerous photographs of some art by Lazarus Beets, an artist from the Bahamas. James explained to John that he and Lazarus went to college and had even exhibited together. James invited John to get together with him while in New Mexico, but in reality James never showed up.

Upon exiting The South West Chief train and entering the Albuquerque station, John ran smack into Dr. Elliot and Dr. Jeffrey. "Hey there, Doctors," John said and continued, "Did you have a good trip here?"

"It was absolutely magnificent, Mr. Albertson," Dr. Elliot returned, "Though, we do apologize for not making the time to take you up on those cocktails. Please tell us, how effective was your research effort on this train?"

"Well, the research I gathered was quite good, in deed. In fact, most of the riders seem to support my thesis that riding Amtrak is a viable and necessary therapeutic resource. Oh, and by the way, would both of you please accept these six miniature bottles of assorted tequila as a token of my regard for the friendship we established. I'm sure at some point during your relaxation, you may find use for them. Please," John said extending the package to them.

With many thanks, they took John's gift, bid hasty farewells, and hurried off in their long black limousine. John, who had only one night to rest at Albuquerque's cheap American Youth Hostel called **Route 66**, had a lot to reflect on.

On this beautiful crisp clear late spring day, John actually felt proud of himself and greatly relieved. He had evidenced two realities: First of all, that the creation of one very skilled psychiatrist was wrapped-up in an abnormal abundance of pain. And secondly, that onboard Amtrak was indeed a useful counseling site of choice. Therefore, with two subjects in the bag, there certainly had to be two more willing subjects waiting to be bagged. It was time to go get them.

THE LOAD

This was the beginning of a cloudless picture-perfect day in Eleuthera Island of the Bahamas—no rain in sight. Sweet tropical breezes gently caressed divinity in the sun-darkened wrinkled faces of many piously nodding elders. And the other nosey old garlic-stinking early-risers—those who had once again triumphed over death, arthritis, high blood pressure and uncertainty along those lonely passages of the night—celebrated life by briskly raking their yards clean in the advancing brilliant light.

There was eighty-four year old Mr. Wilson who hardly ever slept a wink, so as not to miss anything. I mean, any juicy gossip that was flying by real fast. Yet he held his head up high as the only man of his time who never told a single lie, from cradle to grave. Now, you and I both know there was only one perfect man. Or so they say. So we'd wink to each other and let him slide on that one. See, if the truth be told, most of us would rather miss him than see him on a daily basis. But he ain't dead yet, so you know what that means…just silently accept his madness. And since Mr. Wilson was always prying into other people business, he had all the ill-fated news first. Our Johnny on the spot knew everything 'bout everything. He knew who was doing what to whom, how they were doing it, if it was good to them, when they stopped doing it and how it was going to turn out. My God...what a disgusting man!

Now then, there was them ninety-two year old twin sisters, Kathy and Maggie. Mercilessly, that Kathy was forever forcing someone up in her house to drink some damned purple tea. In Jesus' name, she'd be calling out to the master to guide her in her healing work. She would give 'em a big bag with one-month supply of teas to drink, for one illness or another she had pried out of a poor trapped soul. And you'd have to take the tea and use it or else something strange would happen to ya. Oh yeah. And when you used that tea properly, your pee would turn blue for 'bout four weeks straight.

Now after Kathy was finished with you, Maggie would corner you for another half an hour or so and make you listen to what she called singing the Caribbean blues. "Le' me tell ya," she would bellow on and on rhythmically slapping a tin plate for effect, for what felt like 'bout two hours. And good sense would tell ya not to move till she was finished, while you were under the intense scrutiny of both of those sister's four grayish-green searing-hot cat-like eyes. That's if you know what's good for ya.

Oh yes. There was that hell, fire, and brimstone breathing old Ms. Sanders, who everyone tried their best to sidestep. She acted like she was "the way, the truth and the light". Of course, there was that one twitching red and one slack gray-eyed, wise old Uncle John. He comically smiled at you all the time, proudly displaying the only two teeth he had left in his head—one upstairs and the other downstairs, front gum row, center left. Deep inside yourself, you wanted to start laughing in his face about his disturbing features, without stopping till tomorrow this same time. But I tell ya man, he would have licked you with he rose wood walking cane until he died right there on the spot from exhaustion…and probably you would have been dead too. See, he was a proud and serious 85-year-old man with a suspicious wife, Becky—ten years older than he was. Despite his age, Uncle John was still the town's only cobbler, fixing them pretty young women's shoes for them on the double: some faster than others. Once or twice an infuriated Becky caught a sweet young thing showing off their legs and giving Uncle John a sneak peek upon request. It was then that Becky had let go of all her pent up frustrations in that one moment, verbally castigating and cutting him down to size. Deep in thought shortly thereafter, Uncle John had stitched his hand to something leather he was fixing, or sent a nail through a finger; normally that was what happened twice each year, after he and Becky had had their two major fights over the low repair prices he was charging those hot young heifers. And of course, there were the Porters, the Bowlegs, the Thompson twins, Uncle Glen, Aunt Liz, Ma Bethel, Sister Cox and a few more weird seniors, all well past seventy and refusing to die.

Begrudgingly, some of those old folks awoke from their memories mad and others glad, when Green Castle High School's obtrusive three o'clock bell rang. Immediately, throngs of giddy, beautiful brown children heading home surged down the village's main street. For a few minutes each day, I was one of those children heading home. My name is Ida Molten. I had to live this story first before I could step away from it, slide to the right side with it, play hopscotch with it, jump back and shake it loose to the left. I simply had to allow the passing of time, fury and passion to carouse down through my grinding body, invigorating my fingers as I sat down on it and wrote this story pure and simple. This is my message to you.

***

"Good evening, Granny," said 11 year old Ida, as she stepped up onto the porch in her starched-stiff school uniform. "How are you feeling today, Ma?"

"Oh just fine child. I'm ma just a-setting here studying 'bout how stupid we people is. See, everybody go 'round talking and writing 'bout Master John this and Master John that. And how he had his way with we colored island women them, back then. Well, it wasn't so. As always, there are them few black ones that wanted something for free, and don't nothing come for free...child, remember that. Ha, baby," said Mother Bethel patting the upturned bucket's bottom, "But that ain't even half the real story."

Ida immediately recognized that signal to sit down, for there was definitely something very heavy on Granny's mind. However, she played dumb and by choice she remained standing and braced herself to receive a long-winded story. Listen here...see, in them in them Islands there, the elders were treated like earthly Gods or teachers who were unquestioningly honored, obeyed, and respected—always.

Expertly, mother Bethel sprayed tobacco juice over her left shoulder, just barely clearing the banister and promptly dried her lips with that deep brown stained-up handkerchief, she kept stuffed in her bosom. "Ida, darling, set yourself down so I can teach you 'bout life, 'bout sweetness, and 'bout the big mix-up between colored and white people them. I'm gonna tell you what you'll never see in them black history books you bin toting 'round with ya."

Without a way to escape, Ida halfheartedly slumped down onto the over-turned five-gallon bucket by Granny's right side. For no matter how young or old you became, no one ever said no to Ma Bethel, when she was ready to carry-on.

146

Ninety-eight year old great grandmother Bethel seldom told stories, but when she did, they always left an indelible mark on the listener. Most of the time, Granny would start off telling stories from her grandmother Effie about slavery, then she'd work up through early freedom, colored people problems and into our day. Ma Effie, who was no slouch, according to Ma Bethel, lived to be a respectable ninety years of age. We are easily talking about hearing true stories at least one hundred and eighty years old. "Ida, sweetie, would you go get Ma a glass of water, please? God gonna bless ya for it…"

"Yes Madame," said one dejected looking Ida heading straight for the kitchen, feeling somewhat put upon, because she had her own plans on how she wanted to spend this evening, when reality slapped her in the face. "Oh, Ma, I must beg excuse. See I've got to hang up my school uniform so the pleats them stay fresh and in place for tomorrow. Will you please give me couple minutes to change-up?"

"Sure Ida darling and think about this as you go 'long. There ain't no such thing as colored people history or black history just records of people, British, Dutch, French, Spanish, American, black, white, yellow, pink and brown, all messing-up big-time on God's green earth," said Mother Bethel, with a chuckle and a split-second discharge of tobacco juice. "It's sad to say so, but true, we is all one. And the only things that ever come between us in life is knowledge, sex and money"

"Here you are Ma," said Ida handing over the water in Granny's favorite white tin mug.

"Thank ya, Sweetie. Now what I'm 'bout to tell you, we don't tell them silly men folks. This here is purely woman talk. You understand, don't ya, Sweetie?"

"Yes Ma. It's just like you always say, with pride we bear the pain so together we can gain—as women!"

"That's right gal. The future belong to we. Well now, in those days there were great big salt ponds to be worked and plantations to kept up, not only here in the Bahamas or America, but in Haiti, Jamaica, Barbados, Trinidad, Antigua and the whole Caribbean. And even though they say that slavery in the British West Indies ended in 1833, as quiet as it was kept, slavery was still in full force till 'bout 1910. Any time the Queen, some Prince, Princess or royalty was 'bout to visit, at the point of a gun, they made us swear to act as if we were free people, rented out for profit to the plantation owners. We didn't have big money or guns, so we went along in prayer. But the women folk them united and were keen on learning as much as they could and sharing it just with the other no nonsense women them. We started stealing books from Master's library and we began to read and write with help from Master's children them, home on holiday during the summer. Us women had a saying between we self, 'each one teach one'. Child, the men them were too busy laughing or being strong and stupid, to listen to we instructions, 'specially so when they got that strong firewater up in 'em. And if there was one thing they could make from almost any kind of old fruits was the homemade moonshine. See they figured all that mattered was that they were bringing home the bacon. But them men forgot they were making babies, in two or three different homes, too. And the babies needed their fathers. Also, as grown men they had a responsibility to cut a better path for their children, than they had." She paused to drink some water and adjust her seating.

"Back in the day, we people were the toughest of the boatloads of slaves from Gorée Island that they couldna break at James town, so we ended up scatter-'bout here in the Caribbean. And in time we got to mingling with the Lucian Indians them and thing like that. Anyway, the cruel treatment we received as freedmen was the same as in official slavery. And since man and woman didn't share what we learned, most of we had nothing. Not a drop of business sense and very little common sense, too. It was all about money. See, Ma Effie saw it and said it was so. So that's how it go. She was a tall pure black proud straight talking woman, with thick pretty long black hair down to the middle of she back. Still and yet jet-black people like we, had to toil in them yam, cassava, potato, sweet potato, sweet pepper, onion, corn, okra, tomato, tobacco, sugar cane and pineapple fields...Lord, from sunrise to sunset." Sadly, she shook her head and somehow seemed to briefly relive in-full the hurt from past pain as strong tremors rippled through her being. Then Ma Bethel viciously shot another batch of tobacco juice clear across the yard.

"Of course, the blacks who had it good were really Master's sons and daughters sired with we black virgins. And too, some of them easy yellow women he could do, when Miss Annie didn't want to. Anyway, it was hard on us field women 'cause only every so often Master would go easy on us, out in that boiling hot sun. Sometimes the heavy bleeders got their first day off when it was period time. The only other ones to get a break were the virgins who caught Master's fancy. See, they would let him squeeze their thighs and rub their stuff for a promise. Not me! Hell no!" She shot a load of tobacco juice with a vengeance almost twelve feet away.

"Well, I gonna tell you this, I was devoted to my sweet boy and we secrets. I remember catching these sixteen ridges on my back here in 1897, to this very day. Oh, my Savior, thank you. I had just turn 14. Come feel here gal, so you can know." Mother Bethel unzipped the back of her dress halfway down exposing hard dark scared tissue ridges.

149

"Oh my Lord, Granny, I'm so sorry, Ma," cried Ida with tears congregating in her eyes and then in waves those warm tears started to bathe her face.

"Child, dry up your eyes them, so I can finish telling you the real deal…My, Lord! Well, Master John came whistling down the sugar cane row I was cutting, with high yellow Boy Willie on his heels. Master bent over and whispered, 'Sugar plum, let me feel see if you as sweet as the cane you cutting,' and he tried to reach he hand under my dress. And Boy Willie quickly put in his two cent, 'You know Master, the blacker the berry, the sweeter the juice.' But I raised my sickle and brought it down with all my might across Master hand, and left it hanging wide open. Boy Willie was a cussing as he stepped up on me with that cat o' nine tail and was beating me real bad. That's when Little Josh, who was my first love, come clear cross the field and whipped Boy Willie within an inch of he life. Well, Master John and Boy Willie with a group of them field hands got even by stretching poor Joshua out on the wooden cross of torture till his death. They say, Boy Willie as ordered, bust-up he backdoor; and them strong men just stood there trembling like spineless sheep. All them just a thinkin' how what they saw, could come to them. After that, they whipped my Joshua to death and hung him by the neck on that cross at the gate of the plantation, till high noon the next day."

As soon as Granny's hugs and soothing touches stemmed Ida's flow of tears, she resumed her lecture. "Ya see, time passed quickly for us blacks in those days, cause many of us didn't live to make 50 year of age. Now, as they say, time heals everything. The truth is almost everything—not everything. See, hell may have no fury like a woman scorned, but let a man catch another man in he wife, then death is the only redemption for all hands concerned. Ida, you know I love you so you better take heed and remember what I am 'bout to tell you, ok?" Granny's load of boiling tobacco juice flew clean across the porch and landed in the middle of the back of one stray dog that was always sneaking around in search of free food.

"Well, Boy Willie had a twin brother we called Boy Blue. They were different as day and night except in they lust for women. And always wanted the best of them at that. I think it started early in their spoiled rotten *conky joe* lives. 'cause rumor had it that they had big equipment and knew how to use it, them two brothers figured they had the run of the Johnson's plantation all for them two: mean Boy Willie was the Head overseer and we church deacon, while kind-hearted Boy Blue was we preacher. Now the way they worked it, Boy Willie was always sniffing like a dog in heat around the field women them quarters. He was very insecure 'bout his color, and couldn't stand to sleep with he yellow women them. Though he married Nettie, a mean-spirited high yellow lazy brute, if ever I saw one. Nine times out of ten when he didn't get one of we, you would hear him walking round outside late at night singing, 'Well I sure ain't white, but I'm alright, 'cause I'm light. And Master gave me the might oh yeah, oh yeah, master gave me the might oh yeah, oh yeah.' And we'd be singing inside, 'Don't turn back on us, that's right, that's right. We'll put your light out tonight, tonight. We'll punch your lights out tonight, tonight. Oh yeah, oh yeah, that's right, that's right!' Child we'd be carrying-on, having big fun. See, he knew better than to go 'round the men quarters after dark, 'cause, them jet-black men wouldda killed him quick under the cover of night. Poor Boy Willie didn't have no friends except for he brother. Actually, Boy blue would let him read the Bible in church and play deacon, some Sundays. Gal, the women them who went with him only did it for the sneeze little favors he passed out from time to time."

"Like what Ma? What kind of little favors?" Ida asked.

151

"Oh, just some small special British imported sweet scented soaps, silk panties (the maids stole from Miss Annie for him), and pieces of jewelry he said he happened to come by." Ma said with a chuckle. Then she paused to drink some water, catch her breath, and sling some juice.

"Good evening, Ma Bethel. Hi Ida!" shouted 12 year old Leroy Roll bringing his bicycle to an abrupt halt by the porch's steps, for he had a strong crush on Ida, "Say Ida, let's go down to the creak in about thirty minutes, ok?"

"Leroy, look what you done, done! You just cut cross Granny when she was telling a serious story. Apologize right this minute! Now! Do it!" said Ida baring her teeth and balling up both fist menacingly.

"Oh, Granny, I humbly apologize Ma. Will you please pardon me?"

"You're excused this time child. But always mind your manners, son. Don't be in such a hurry, child. There is plenty of life yet for you to live. Now run along till I finish talking personal to Ida." Leroy did not linger a second longer than he had to. Quickly he turned his bicycle around and sped away.

"If the truth be told, Bible-toting Boy Blue was a sweetheart with we dark girls and the plantation owner's number one pimp. Well, through no fault of he own, he found out that Miss Annie was tired of Master John in she bedroom. Miss Annie heard them yellow gals talking 'bout how big and sweet Boy Blue's equipment was and curiosity got the best of her. She was up early one Sunday morning at dawn and got dressed all prettied-up in laces and frills. She convinced Master John into believing that she had go to the colored folks Easter Sunday church service, as a sign of their love and commitment as slave owners to Jesus. This was a show of Christian good faith 'wards the slaves. And see, Master quickly came round to her line of thinking after she let him eat her bread; I mean her nookie, child, reassuring him for 'bout half hour. So Master John and Boy Willie, we part time deacon, drove Miss Annie to church. Then they sat smoking cigars and talking in the truck outside, while colored folks Bible service was raging on like a wild fire inside." Ma quickly shot some thick black steamy hot tobacco juice clear across the yard and missed their black cat by inches.

"Well, all was fine as Miss Annie sat up in the front row going 'long with the service, until she hitched up her dress so high that Boy Blue and the choir saw nothing but her bare nookie, facing him fair and square. And she had the nerve to act as if it was an accident when Boy Blue's eyes grew big as a saucer. And for a moment, he lost he tongue. Sister Mary Johnson jumped straight up out of her front row choir seat and shouted "Let the house say amen, amen, amen, amen!" Quickly, before everybody caught-on she hugged Boy Blue and led the church in prayer, a prayer that lasted almost ten minutes. Let me tell you one thing child, what you sow, you're gonna reap, before you leave this earth. I done seen it come true too many times, gal." Granny paused to fix herself better on her seat, knowing full well that she had Ida hooked on her true story.

"And so it was. Boy Blue started sleeping with Miss Annie. She fell in love with him. The reasons were simple enough for a fool to understand. In her fantasy, she always wanted to be treated like how colored girls were treated, by Master, but with equipment the size of what she heard Boy Blue had. When Master left early in the morning, Boy Blue would put the wood to her and you would hear Miss Annie a-shouting "Tear me up Blue, oh do me Baby, oh Lord do me, Jesus! Yes! You're busting me up, but don't stop!" All the trusted house hands would exchange winks and roar with laughter quickly hushed, but never did they breathe a word of this to anyone. Then you would hear Boy Blue's pockets full of silver shillings making noise as he was leaving down the back stairs. Oh yeah, she used to treat him real good. She would give him money and the best of her jewelry. After that, Miss Annie would come down stairs all flushed, carefree, and smiling like nothing had happened, singing her little heart out. For almost two year this went on right under Master's nose." Ma quickly stuck a fresh pinch of tobacco up between her cheeks…and you could see her spirits rise.

"It happen that 'bout two week before May Day, Master John started looking at his Miss Annie funny. In fact, he told her sternly, in front of all of we, to start taking more walks and stop eating so much. At the same time, Miss Annie figured out that this was the second month she had missed her period. Now, just for pretense sake they slept in the same room each night, even though Miss Annie had not had her husband since last Christmas. She loathed him for trying to touch her or for even looking at her with lust in he eyes. There was too much wrong with that picture. First, there was two rascals worried about how to deal with the grape-vine rumors 'bout Miss Annie's morning sickness and possible pregnancy. And a husband who didn't have a clue, so, he considered his wife lazy and getting fat from eating too much. See, it seemed like by right Boy Blue should have been declared the true father. Not so! Because, whenever Boy Blue felt an attack of he stomach ulcers coming on, and Miss Annie needed some loving, he worked it out so Boy Willie covered for him. At first Boy Willie would fix up a dark girl, a virgin or a good actress, to spend a day with Master at their private beach house. That left Willie in charge of them field hands, and with plenty room to go and give Miss Annie that cruel type of loving she craved, without her realizing the difference." Ma Bethel paused to dispense with some juice and sip some water.

"Both brothers' hands were dirty. Each with he blame, tried to cover-up he shame. We just laughed 'bout it. 'cause, if ever you caught them boys eyes for a split second, you would see pure guilty in 'em. See, Boy Willie's other duty was to punish rebel girls who Master wanted to sleep with, but wouldn't give in. On cue they would drag that gal down to the whipping shed. And four strong men would hold her down while Willie bust-up her insides. See gal, Master had a small pecker, so he couldn't do no damage. And most of the time he just wanted to eat it, anyway."

"Inquiries were made by Miss Annie for Sibyl, the local roots woman, to come and make her abort. She was gonna have to quickly lose that black baby in her. But Sibyl was too scared to take such a big chance and get involved. Willie just wanted this mess to be over like yesterday. But he couldn't stop going over and standing in for he brother. Meanwhile, Boy Blue's stomach was acting up on him almost every day now, and Miss Annie was starting to feel like she was being betrayed by not seeing enough of Boy Blue. In fact, she started talking crazy talk 'bout leaving Master. Miss Annie with she money, had figured on carrying the load of her disgrace, the baby, and Boy Blue, far away. Somewhere in Europe she figured would be best. Then they could all live as one big respectable middle class family, in peace." Granny spat some more juice that landed on the banister this time and on a sly, looked around to see if Ida had noticed.

Ida was a very smart young woman and played like she was tying her shoes and didn't see a thing. The unspoken rules were you never did anything to make your Granny feel small. So Granny felt safe and began again, "Sweetie, there are three types of women in this world when it comes down to man, equipment, and money. There is that plain humble sweet woman that looks for and takes a husband as security and company for life. No matter how he look she'll take him, so long as he is hard-working, kind-hearted, will ride her well, eat her often and can laugh at himself. Them two have a good chance of living long and happily together, 'cause he'll work hard and let her manage the money, mostly. And she'll stay at home and raise the children till they can do for themselves. That's when she'll get herself a job or some community work till they choose to retire together. Child, that's the good life. That type of man you have to grow up with and train him from day one. Just like you doing with that Leroy. Make him toe the line as far as respect is concern. Keep him in line. He might do you some good, some day." She stopped, took her brown spotted handkerchief out and wiped away the sweat that had congregated on her forehead.

"The next type of woman is the one who is strong-minded like a man and too selfish to mother a child. She'll get all the worldly things she desire out of life by deception, lies, and the sale of her body. Her goal is to get to be in charge of something big. She always has to dress up like a star, in a world that only exist in a dream. She'll be in charge alright, but yet still, a lonely old bitch behind closed doors playing with herself. She'll forever feel used-up and truly unloved regardless of all her money. She might just as easily turn funny after looking down her "better" nose at all the male hands that come after she. Sorry to say it, but, she will never achieve any real satisfaction in a relationship based on a give and take basis. And Ida, gal, that will spell a short life span for her. Believe me, life is too short to chase after your tail. Don't be puffed up with pride waiting forever, 'cause there ain't no Mister right coming looking for you after a certain age. Child, don't take other women hard luck stories 'bout men to heart or you'll turn out just like them. Believe me, they did more for their bad luck than they're letting on to you."

"The last type is the bright love child, who need to hear sweet nothings all the time—every night. She selects her men based on the size of their hands, feet, and the size of their equipment. A very insecure and deadly woman, that one is, 'cause she is hooked on not sleeping alone. Child, that heifer will walk up in your house and take your man without notice. That brute is always on the hunt for the biggest equipment she can find. Nine times out of ten she is barren or well on the way to being barren—that's after her insides have been chew-up enough. That slut will gladly live in a matchbox with a lazy man that has the right size equipment. She'll ask for nothing but good loving from him and will work hard to buy him everything he owns and wants by obligation. But her downfall is that you can't buy loving forever. Sooner or later there will be a bigger attraction and that man will be gone. All I'll say to you is that you must have self-respect and discipline. And remember, it's not the size of the ship but the motion of the ocean that will give you sweetness."

Granny paused grinning at Ida, who was all wide eyed and looking like she was in a trance. "And keep this one to yourself. Don't ever fully trust any woman, not even your mother, with your man. She'll be with him in a minute. Women are treacherous and men are not strong when it comes to sweetness. But still, you can trust a man any day within reason 'cause he only want some nookie. Hell, he'll lie to get some satisfaction from you, but in fact you'll find a true friend in him quicker than in any woman. And too, you can always tell a good man no, and he will wait respectfully looking forward to the time when you will say yes." She shot some tobacco juice, drank some water and just sat rocking and hugging herself for a few long moments, chuckling.

"Oh my, child, I know I must have gone off the deep end, so, bear with me while I get back to we story. Well, it was Friday the first day of August when the truth finally came out. I'll never forget that day 'cause it was the day I was brought up from the fields to fix gumbo. Nobody on that plantation could cook gumbo like me. But I was too dark-colored and proud to be head cook or even live in the big house. Boy Willie was up there plowing in Ms. Annie like nobody's business, when Master John came in on them. See, Master John had started to feel something fishy was going on, but couldn't quite put he finger on it. Anyway, he was at the beach house that day with Sarah, when the thought hit him that maybe there was someone else, and he got real sick in he stomach. He told Sarah to relax until he got back 'cause he was going to pick some tealeaves for the stomach cramps he was having. He stopped first at the plantation and there was no Boy Willie there. He parked his truck about quarter mile away. And by dodging behind trees and bushes, he made it up the back stairs with his rifle in hand and kicked down the bedroom door. Everybody froze stiff for a good two minutes in shock. Then all Hell broke loose. Well, Master John didn't out-smart Lightfoot Miller, who was right behind him with a cricket bat, ready. So, soon as Master caught his senses and raised the gun to shoot Miss Annie and Boy Willie, Lightfoot took the bat and knocked him cold. Cradling the gun, Lightfoot made Tommy James, the butler, hog-tie an angry but pleading Boy Willie. Next, Master John was placed in a steel chair to which Tommy tied his right arm and left leg properly. That's when Ma Effie came in from the shed with a basin of cold water and some spirits of ammonia to revive whoever needed it. And, of course, there was me with my big spoon in hand coming from the kitchen, hot on Ma Effie's heels." Granny paused as two large noisy trucks passed by.

"Child, what a melee. There was Miss Annie calling Boy Willie Boy Blue and Boy Willie screaming to Miss Annie that he was not Boy Blue. And a confused Master John was a shouting for Boy Willie to stretch out he fingers them. 'Cause only Master knew the secret of these twins lay in their finger count. Now, Boy Willie and Boy Blue had pulled the wool over we eyes since the

158

first time we knew them. They always kept their hands in their pockets. The truth shocked us so to see Boy Willie had six fingers on each hand, which left Miss Annie a bit angry to see that in fact she had really been doing both brothers. Boy Willie swore to her that she never had relations with Boy Blue. He said that he had allowed her to call him Boy Blue since it seemed like that was her fantasy. He just never bothered to straighten her out. That's the only reason, Willie pleaded, why she could have thought he was Boy Blue. Meanwhile, deep down, Boy Willie told this lie hoping to at least get Boy Blue off the hook. Momentarily, Master John was demanding that he be cut loose, immediately, so he could kill Boy Willie with his bare hands." Hot tobacco juice flew its distance as she relaxed briefly.

"Well, the tide quickly changed when Boston Blackboy came barreling in the room knocking Lightfoot out cold. He used a vicious head butt. See, Blackboy was not only the colored-folks boxing champion but also the best wrestler and street fighter on the plantation. Mama had Florence, the maid, ride Miss Annie's bicycle to the field ordering Blackboy to come quick. That was when she saw Lightfoot tipping up behind Master with the cricket bat. Blackboy wasn't too swift upstairs, but at least he knew which side of the fence put the butter on his bread. Most of the time when Boy Willie was not in the field, Blackboy kept the men them working properly. Well, Tommy didn't want to get beat-up, so he quickly did what Blackboy ordered. He cut Master John loose. Master jumped up and snatched the rifle in one motion from Boston Blackboy and slammed six of Miss Annie's front teeth down her throat. Next he ordered everyone outside, at gun point." She slung more juice.

"Now. To make a long story short, Master sent word 'bout two o' clock that morning for Sibyl to come help Miss Annie, 'cause she was bleeding heavy. Lord, my child. Miss Annie was black

159

and blue all over and flowing like a river as she miscarried. We knew it was gonna happen, 'cause we heard him taking turns beating her some then beating Boy Willie some, all night long. So five o'clock that morning, the men took what was left of Boy Willie out to the whipping shed. Master summonsed Boy Blue, who came sweating a death sweat with his Bible under he arm and his preacher collar in place. 'Boy Blue, I'm sorry this had to happen this way,' said Master John tapping his rifle's trigger with his finger, 'Doesn't your holy book say that what a man has done so let it be done unto him? And does it not say that what a man sows so shall he reap?'

'Yes Master, you are perfectly right, Sir.'

'Well then, for all the women and men, them nookies and butts Willie has bust-up. And for disgracing my wife, Boy Blue, I command you to do the same to him.'

'But, Master I.'

'Do it now!' shouted Master, as he cranked and pointed the shotgun threateningly.

'Fair is fair,' said Boston Blackboy, as Master and rifle advanced upon Boy Blue. So Boy Blue, who already had his belongings packed and ready to leave, dropped his britches and pumped his juices in Boy Willie's greased up butt." Granny scrutinized Ida's face then released some more tobacco.

"Child, no sooner than Boy Blue finish tearing up he brother's hind parts, Master spoke-up, 'Well, I can't trust you two boys no more. See, Annie done confessed, she knew all along that she was sleeping with both of you.' He stood thinking for a brief moment then said, 'And if you'll do this to your own brother what can I expect you to do to me, if ever I turn my back? Nothing personal, just precaution.' Master fired two bullets from the double-barrel shot-gun, and both brothers' heads fell to the ground, cut off at the neck."

160

The little ice cream truck came by moving slowly, but neither young nor old woman seemed a bit impressed. Obviously, it was a nuisance that was not welcomed at that specific moment.

"We got word after Miss Annie left that she had turned to alcohol for relief from her grief. But at least she did give Master John a quiet, simple divorce, with complete control over all four children in boarding school." Two loud mouth stray dogs started a fight with the slickest black cat in the neighborhood named Bertha. Bertha quickly ran across the street and up the tambourine tree, after drawing blood from around the left eye of the menacing brown dog. She had easily won again.

"Unfortunately, a good year hadn't passed before the children came home to Miss Annie's funeral. She died from white liver and worrying over regrets that she could not change. It was a shame to see how she gave up so much for so little. Anyway, by then Master had changed the entire plantation around to a freedman's colony. See, Master John Johnson fell in love with Lilly May, the biggest, blackest, hardest heel woman on the plantation. That's right, she knew how to cry-out loud and hard and make Master feel like he was able to do something great with he little pecker in her butt. Then he upped and married her. I tell you girl, he made all them high yellow women servants—those who wanted to keep their old jobs for a salary—jump to the new Madame Lilly May's every beck and call. Now, they didn't like that one bit, but at least they were making honest money. Most of the other black women them were allowed to buy land and even employed some of the men them with their profits. Soon Lilly May had a free school set up, which educated black women and children to be something important in society. Believe me, child, there is something good that come out of every misfortune."

Granny tensed up and frowned, shocked to see the 4:30pm bus stop across the street and the day workers getting off. Time had flown by so fast. "Oh, baby, quickly straighten up the house, before your Ma get home."

"And thank you so very much for making me more wise, Granny," said Ida applying a quick kiss to Granny's right cheek, as she cheerfully trotted off.

"You're welcome, sweet baby! And don't forget 'bout your homework, darlin'." Granny yelled after her.

Gulfrey Clarke earned a business degree in the first graduating class of the University of the District of Columbia (WTI) Washington. D.C. 1977, before attending the USDA Graduate School of Business.

He withdrew from Howard University to practice accounting and pursue independent research opportunities in American-Caribbean trade policies, relationships, treaties and MOUs.

In The Bahamas he wrote letters to the editors concerning economic policies and living conditions in 1980.

He is the author of two memoirs: *Aquamarine Blues* and *An American Nightmare*. And now Mr. Clarke takes great pride and pleasure in releasing his first collection of short stories entitled: *Blues In Small Dose*.

Gulfrey is a proud father of three and grandfather of four, who finds time for aikido, creative writing, table tennis and portrait or landscape oil painting, between English teaching engagements.

He has managed his Steady Steps English School for ten years using TEFL and CELTA English teaching qualifications from Cambridge University along with a Swiss SVEB 1 add on module; and taught English in Zurich and Bern Switzerland for fifteen years.

To review a few of the author's letters to the editor of the Nassau Guardian in 1980, his full bio or copies of the press releases associated with all of his works published by Cocoon Publishers, do feel free to visit his website: gulfreyc//.wix. gulfreyclarke.

73787668R00104

Made in the USA
Columbia, SC
18 July 2017